Pacifica

The Revelation Trilogy
Book One

T.E. Burrell

DEDICATION

The Revelation Trilogy is dedicated to the two women who made it possible.

My mother, Mickey, FORCED me to read for an hour every day during my summer break between first and second grade. It started an obsession that I am forever grateful for.

My wife, Becky, supplied an amazing level of patience and understanding along the journey. Those who know me well can attest this is no small feat. Without her advice and support, this story would still be rolling around in my head all by itself.

CONTENTS

Acknowledgements

1 Survey   1
2 Apple Falls   3
3 Archery Practice   11
4 School Project   19
5 Recess   25
6 Volunteer Commander   27
7 Friday Night Bonfire   35
8 Dinner at the Inn   41
9 Invitation   49
10 Obligation   59
11 Celebration   63
12 Angus   73
13 In Hell   79
14 Freshmen Orientation   93
15 After Hell   99
16 Induction Ceremony   121
17 Guard Education   129
18 Blue Heron Tavern   135
19 Gloria   145
20 Diana's Hunt   159
21 Invasion   167
22 Council Vote   177
23 Mobilization   189
24 Peace Negotiations   201
25 The Wall, Day 1   213
26 The Wall, Day 2   227
27 The Wall, Day 3   235
28 The Wager   243
29 Hall of Heroes   245
30 Solitude   253
31 Improving the Odds   259

ACKNOWLEDGEMENTS

My thanks to Jordan for his insightful feedback, questions, ideas, and encouragement during the writing of this trilogy. His developmental editing was incredibly helpful.

Thanks also to Jess and Emmaleigh for their help with the cover art. Their advice, energy, and creativity is greatly appreciated by someone who is significantly artwork challenged.

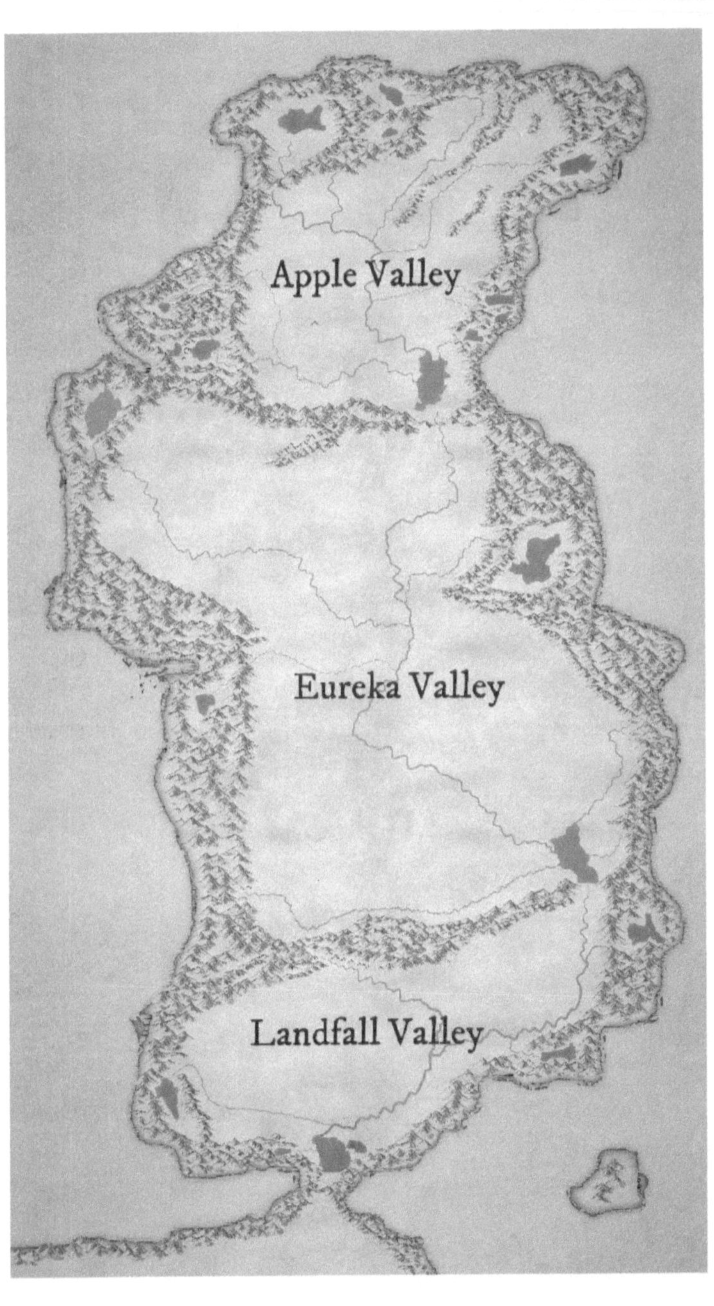

Apple Valley
Eureka Valley
Landfall Valley

CHAPTER 1

SURVEY

"These people have no idea what is about to hit them," the anthropologist said quietly to himself. The ocean planet below was a beautiful blue. The single large landmass directly below him had a few swirls of white above it, but was mostly clear. He was observing two primitive civilizations from an altitude of twenty-five hundred kilometers.

His survey ship and its network of satellites had a wide and diverse array of sophisticated surveillance equipment. The instruments could visually zoom in with incredible resolution and even listen in on conversations given the right atmospheric conditions. Grant Parson could peer into the intimate private lives of the people below while remaining completely anonymous and invisible.

These primitive cultures were living in an inhospitable world. They had evolved to thrive in spite of the challenges. But each had lost their technology since emigrating from Earth nearly two millennia ago. The mutants were slowly but surely assembling an enormous horde. They would soon overwhelm the true humans. It would be a massacre.

This was unfortunate in Grant's mind. So many interesting things to study and time was running out. But he was excited about the carnage that was soon to come.

Because he was an anthropologist, he felt he had the inside track on how this would play out. He had already placed a large bet. The true humans' main line of defense would fail in the next battle. He would be rich! Grant was looking forward to multiple days of live streamed watch parties, followed by his payout. It would be memorable.

Stuck in a survey ship out in the middle of nowhere was not the exciting life Grant had envisioned as an anthropologist. He sometimes regretted his choice of profession. But having a front-row seat to this spectacle was worth all the long and lonely hours.

CHAPTER 2

APPLE FALLS

Del could hear Apple Falls before he could see them. Rounding a bend in the road, he stopped to admire the stark beauty of the main waterfall. It was still a long way off, but the sound of the falling water already drowned out everything else. It never ceased to make him homesick. He had moved away to attend university many years ago. He would likely never move back.

Del was Dean of Landfall University and enjoyed his work and his life. But he still got homesick. As he got nearer to the falls, the power of the enormous volume of water seemed to press in from all sides. This was the first of three falls that rose a combined eighteen hundred feet above the Eureka Valley. He thought the view from the top of the falls was the prettiest place in all of Pacifica.

Del was tall, broad, olive-skinned, and of late, a bit portly. An ordinary man with the exception of his eyes. It wasn't the color or size that caught your attention; it was their intensity.

It was a bright, brisk morning, and Del had been up early. He was enjoying the hike alongside the turbulent Apple River leading to the falls. Having spent the previous night in a small village inn he had started his day well rested. His mood alternated between joy at the beauty of the hike and berating himself for not exercising more often. He could feel his back, knees, and leg muscles as he labored up the road. Even more troubling was his heavy breathing. He was ashamed. Middle age and the sedentary nature of a university professor had taken its toll.

There was a strong bias among his people to stay in excellent physical condition. Pacifica had been in a long-standing and brutal war between the peninsula and the continent for well over a thousand years. Everyone was expected to be prepared to serve as a soldier at a moment's notice. His position as university dean meant his direct participation in the fighting was extremely unlikely. But everyone was expected to be able to contribute to the common defense.

Traversing the Falls was the only way to enter the Apple Lakes region. This region was located at the tip of a peninsula. It consisted of a main valley that was both long and wide. A deep lake fed the falls at one end. The main valley was surrounded by mountains on the other three sides that plunged steeply from cliffs into the ocean. Arranged like a fan were a half dozen smaller valleys with their own lakes and waterfalls draining into the central valley. These smaller valleys were sparsely populated and purposely not developed. Apple Lakes was a natural fortress. It was the last line of defense for Pacifica. There had to be room to expand if the worst occurred.

Del was on his way to evaluate two students at the Apple Lake's school for admission to the university. It was unusual for more than one applicant from this rural region to be accepted. Many years there were none. Del suspected the local teacher might be guilty of overstating her student's capabilities.

Given they were Dr. Dorothy Esper's twins, she could be excused for perhaps being a bit overwhelmed by their mother. He had high regard for the teacher, who had been a recent university graduate. A teacher being overly enthusiastic about her students was not unusual nor a bad thing. If Del found even one of them qualified for university entry, the trip would be well worth it. If not, it would be a good learning experience for the young teacher.

Del thought teachers ought to aggressively advocate for their students. He would be warm and supportive with his mentoring, regardless of how the applications for admittance worked out. He knew he had a reputation for being intimidating. So, he needed to take special care to not dampen a young teacher's enthusiasm.

His plan was to avoid climbing the long narrow switchback trail that snaked its way up alongside the Apple Falls's lowest and largest waterfall. It rose eleven hundred feet above the Eureka Valley floor and was a very challenging hike. This plan took on more significance once he realized how badly out of shape he had become. The trail alongside the falls took advantage of a natural cleft in the sheer granite wall.

The cleft made a trail possible up this lowest section of the waterfall. From there, a proper road was available that snaked its way up the steep incline past the two upper falls that were much less daunting. It must have taken many years and enormous effort to chisel out the narrow path to the top of the lower falls. He planned to avoid the arduous climb by riding the Tram.

The Tram was a recent marvel of Pacifica engineering. Del participated in the design portion of the project by providing historical examples of trams and assisting the responsible engineer in calculating stresses and safety margins. It was water powered and comprised of a complex system of cables, pulleys, clutch, and brakes.

Technologies that were commonplace to his ancestors.

The surviving accounts described the Colony Wars as so devastating that civilization was lost for a time. His people had gone from traversing the galaxies to engaging every ounce of energy they had in the struggle to grow enough food. The fact their civilization had survived at all was a miracle. Del was proud of this step forward.

The Tram investment was justified by its ability to transport fruit, lumber, and metals from the Apple Lakes region to the two larger and more densely populated valleys below. Apples, plums, peaches, and sweet cherries were grown in abundance in the Apple Lakes Valley. Their export to the lower two regions was a vital part of Pacifica's food supply.

In return, Apple Lakes received manufactured goods and a variety of grains, including rice, wheat, barley, and corn. A secondary motivation for the Tram was that the Apple Lakes region was the last redoubt for their people. This uplifted portion of the end of the peninsula formed a perfect defensive castle for the region. Care had been taken to ensure it could be self-sufficient if needed. It could end up being critical for their very survival.

As Del strolled over to the Tram, a booming voice called out from behind him. "DELLLLL." He slumped down a bit as a deep sinking feeling appeared in his stomach. He knew his plan to take the Tram was gone. "You're not thinking of risking your life on that ill-conceived death trap, are you?"

Del turned and looked back toward the voice. Walking toward him was Griff. An extremely robust man with a closely shaven head, dark eyes, and copper colored skin that advertised a lifetime spent outdoors. Even when speaking in a conversational tone, Griff's voice carried everywhere.

"I know the Tram is difficult to understand. I know it's scary. Try and show a little courage," Del said, motioning toward the Tram operator and group of men loading it who had stopped to watch them. "And no, I am not riding the Tram. I am going to have it take my backpack to the top." If he had to hike to the top, he was damned if he was going to carry a heavy backpack up the trail, too.

"Call me coward, but I am smart enough to know certain death when I see it," Griff bellowed with a harsh laugh. "I'm not going to risk my change of underwear to that rickety contraption either," Griff boomed and chuckled some more.

Griff could be accused of many things, but a coward wasn't one of them. He was Master Sergeant of the Guard. The Guard was Pacifica's elite group of professional full-time warriors and there was only one master sergeant. While every citizen of Pacifica were part time warriors, the Guard was its base for strategy, training, leadership, and special assignments. Griff's rank was not ceremonial. In battle, he was often in the front line. Typically, in the most vulnerable position. Between wars, he was responsible for guiding recruitment and training.

Griff was short for a member of the Guard, which Del knew he was a bit sensitive about. But he was massively built with a reputation for being quick as a panther. Once Griff got inside your Guard, the fight was over. And he always got inside your Guard. Only Vic had been held in higher regard. Vic was legendary, nearly a deity in Guard lore. He was the previous master sergeant and had been Griff's mentor. Vic was the one fighter Griff could never best. Vic simply disappeared one day twenty years ago, adding to the reverence.

Anyone observing this would wonder if these two were old friends or bitter enemies. Del knew Griff was pretending to be suspicious of the Tram. He was also publicly giving him a pass on having to cart his heavy backpack up the switchback trail. While neither would ever admit it to the other, there was long-standing respect and trust between the two. They were friends. They had met twenty years ago when Griff was a Newbie attending a Guard required history of warfare course at the university. Del was a graduate student teaching the course.

When Del announced the required reading, Griff asked with his affected 'slow learner' facial expression and voice, "Does that big book have anything useful in it?" As if that were a serious question.

"Only if you know how to read," replied Del, staring him down. They held the stare for several seconds until Del said while still looking at him, "Any more stupid questions?"

Griff just grinned back at him. There weren't many that were brave enough to stare Griff down. The clash of egos continued to this day but had mellowed as friendship and respect slowly overtook their competitive natures.

Del knew Griff was intelligent, even if he did consistently play the fool around university staff for fun. In his training role, Griff had worked with Del to develop specialized university classes for the Guard. They both saw benefit to their partnership. Some of the university professors privately scorned the Guard, believing they should just stick to fighting and leave education and decision making to those better suited for it.

"Why the trip to Apple Lake?" Del asked. He knew it was either to evaluate the defensive capabilities of the region or for recruitment.

"Heard there's a boy showing promise for the Guard. His father was accepted into recruit training but didn't make the cut. Rumor is he's been training the boy his entire life to accomplish what he couldn't." Griff paused, then asked, "How about you, recruitment visit?"

"Yeah, it's that time of year," Del replied.

"Given the history of Apple Lakes scholars, I would think you would be looking elsewhere," Griff said with the corners of his mouth slightly upturned. He knew Del had been born and raised in the Apple Lakes.

Del ignored the good-natured dig and said, "There are two candidates the local teacher has referred. I'll spend the week looking over their work, discuss their potential with the teacher, and decide if either merit an invitation."

"Well, looks like I'm going to have to put up with you for a few days," Griff commented and then turned and started up the trail.

Del smiled, admitting that a few days with Griff would be professionally useful and privately enjoyable. He sighed deeply, synched up his belt, and grimly followed.

CHAPTER 3

ARCHERY PRACTICE

Tee was running ten feet behind Diana on a well-used trail that wound its way through the trees. They were headed to the last station for today's training. There was a long-standing agreement that Diana would take the lead when a fast pace was required. Tee was the faster runner, and this ensured the quickest pace while still keeping them together as a team. It also supplied Tee with the guilty pleasure of admiring Diana's butt. Which, in his opinion, had much to be admired. They broke out into the clearing and discovered their last stage. The target was sixty yards away on a hill above them.

Diana grabbed one of the two bows at the station, notched an arrow, pulled back, and placed it just inside the red circle. Tee had simultaneously pulled back as well, centering on the bullseye. Then he almost imperceptibly adjusted his aim and launched an arrow. It landed just outside the red circle. They had both launched second arrows before the first ones had landed. These were both inside the bullseye.

"You win, Diana," Tee said with a groan.

"You're getting worse, or you just let me win," she responded with a smile that included a question in her voice and on her face.

Tee threw up his hands and said, "No, you won fair

and square." An electric smile replaced the questioning one with her obvious pleasure at besting him. It was worth the lie. Diana was tall, robustly athletic, and had a smile that exploded onto her face when she was amused. Tee glanced up and caught his mother frowning at him. She knew he had intentionally lost and then lied about it. It was also possible she saw where his attention had been when they came into the clearing. He would get an earful later tonight.

Diana was one of his oldest friends and his mother's protégé. But she was not the archer he was. His mother was the only one who could beat him. She was Lead Archer for the Apple Lakes Volunteers and perennial winner of the yearly archery competition in the Pacifica Games. Arti was a legend in Apple Lakes.

Being a small rural community, there was great civic pride in her winning the archery competition year after year. The Pacifica Games were based on a wide range of abilities and skills related to warfare. Arti was a name known throughout Pacifica for her dominance with that weapon of war.

Almost all the winners in the fighting skills events were members of the Guard. But it was not unusual for the foot races, weightlifting, and archery events to be won by regular citizens. Women dominated the archery competitions. That domination came partly from a belief that archery was for women and old men. Boys and young men concentrated on hand-to-hand combat. Their weapons were sword, knife, and spear. Skills that were needed for battle on and below the Wall.

Arti had decided today's last challenge was to take them through a running course with random bows at each of ten stations. These bows had a variety of draw weights. The objective was to run up to each station, gauge the bow with the first arrow, then be precise enough to place the second arrow in a small red circle anywhere from ten to seventy-five yards away. For this exercise, Arti required the second arrow to be loosed within three seconds of the first. It took much practice to do this accurately. The wind tended to pick up and swirl in the late afternoon, making it all the more challenging. Tee thought his mother was a bit obsessed with unlikely scenarios.

For today's challenge, her argument was that chaos was a common condition on the Wall and if your bow was damaged, you needed to quickly grab another and be accurate. Tee had to admit that with practice not only could he get his second arrow in the circle, but his first arrow more often than not hit dead center. His mother was always coming up with unique challenges.

Arti looked sternly at Tee and said, "Diana and I are going to walk the course a second time. You can go down to the lake if you want, but be home by suppertime."

"See you down at the beach later, Tee," Diana said with an amused smile still in place.

Tee smiled back and just raised his hand in acknowledgement as they walked back down the trail. His mother dismissing him like that was a rebuke. She had warned him before about letting her other archers beat him. She said it wasn't kindness. "The girls are very competitive," his mother had said again just yesterday. "When you let any of them tie or beat you, it just makes them complacent. There are good reasons why I never let up on you or any of them." Tee had to admit she was probably right. His obsessive practice with the bow was partly driven by wanting to beat his mother. As daunting and elusive as that was.

As Tee entered puberty, he had become more and

more in turmoil around Diana. He loved her as his childhood friend. That had matured into something much more. Lately he had been tongue tied or, worse yet, saying stupid things when she was around. She didn't seem to notice his attraction to her, which was a relief. But it was embarrassing all the same. She was his cousin Ansen's girlfriend. His perfect cousin had the perfect girlfriend. He was jealous. He could admit that. But they were both so caring and kind to 'the freak' that he could not be resentful or angry about it.

You need to stop being delusional, Tee, he thought. They will get married, have beautiful children, and we will all be friends forever. It was a pleasant thought, but the turmoil remained. As his mother and Diana disappeared down the course path, he casually picked up the other bow, notched an arrow, and neatly dropped it dead center in the target.

Tee ran at a fast pace for the three miles to the lake. He arrived breathing easily, but with a sheen of sweat. He took off his clothes until all he had on was a pair of swimming trunks Grammy had made. He dove into the shockingly cold water but acclimated quickly as he swam and fell into a rhythm. Tee's mother knew he needed a swim. Which is why she mentioned the lake. She might be angry with him, but didn't let that interfere with what she knew he needed.

Swimming burned off energy and anxiety like nothing else for Tee. Swimming was an odd thing to be able to do. It often made him a target for bullies. But it was worth it. Quinn and Hestie's mother explained why he could swim so well when others struggled. She was a well-known medical researcher before she converted into one of Apple Valley's family doctors. She had done some research on his unusual ability. Tee was short and slender.

His bone structure, although solid and well formed, was unusually light. He also had a less dense musculature than others. If he relaxed and simply laid on his back, he could actually float in the water. Nobody else could do that. Everyone had to learn to swim. It was so they wouldn't drown if they accidentally fell into the lake. Being able to make it fifty feet was the requirement. Most could barely do that. A normal person dropped to the bottom of the lake if they stopped swimming vigorously.

Dr. Espers had stressed that there wasn't anything wrong with him. He was just different. He overheard her telling his mother that he was a "Throwback."

Years later, in history class, he finally figured out what she meant. He was like the original colonists. Smaller and lighter before they naturally evolved to live on Pacifica. They were initially worried about him breaking bones, but so far that wasn't a problem. His bones were lighter than normal, but strong enough for his frame.

Tee swam to a private beach on the far side of the lake. He thought of the small sandy beach nestled in the cliffs as his. The only way to get there was by boat or to swim. It was a good place to think when he was troubled. Being outside under the sun or stars had always calmed Tee. It was his place to solve problems or control anxiety.

As the sun started to dip, he decided he needed to swim back. When he reached the other side, he saw Hestie standing on the beach. She and her brother were his next-door neighbors and close friends. At first glance, Hestie was a pretty girl, but not someone who stood out in the crowd. However, there was a warmth that emanated from her. She had a way about her that made people instantly like and trust her. The more you got to know Hestie, the more attractive she became.

As Tee stood and started to walk out of the lake, he

raised his hand to wave. Then he noticed Hestie had a worried expression on her face. He realized with a start that Angus and his two brothers were also on the beach. He could tell that they had been harassing Hestie.

"Looky here, a turd washed up on shore," Angus declared to the laughter of his brothers. "You know, people don't float. But turds do. We should bury it. That's the sanitary thing to do, right?"

With that, Angus tackled him and held him while his two brothers dug a hole in the sand. Hestie was pleading with them to stop, but they paid her no mind. They buried him with his arms shoved underneath his legs in a seated position with just his head above the beach. Tee tried to pull his arms out, but the sand was too heavy. He was trapped.

"Show him what we found in the rocks," Angus told the youngest brother. The next thing Tee knew, a Viper snake with its fangs unfolded was being waved in front of his face. Vipers could kill you if you got too much of their venom.

"Leave him alone, Angus!" Tee relaxed, recognizing Ansen's voice.

"Don't ruin all the fun," Angus replied, turning. With that, Diana, Ansen, and Ansen's younger sister Tia walked out of the woods and onto the beach. Ansen was an impressive looking young man. Tall, broad, and muscular, his usual easy-going manner had been replaced with anger. "I said leave him alone."

"It's no big deal. We were just having a little fun with the dwarf." Angus put his face close to Tee and whispered, "You get to float away today, turd, but your cousin won't always be around."

As Ansen walked off, Tia hurried over and said with

concern in her voice, "Are you okay, Tee?"

"Now that you're here to save me, I am," he said, smiling. Tia was Ansen's youngest sister and a joy to everyone. He was horrified that Diana had witnessed this. He hoped he covered it well. Having Ansen save him while Diana watched was especially embarrassing. But having Tia there made it impossible not to smile. "Did you help Aunt Arti up at the archery range?" he asked Tia as Ansen, Diana, and Hestie used their hands to dig him out.

"Yes, I'm retrieving arrows and learning to fix them," Tia said with excitement in her voice. Tia worshipped Diana. She had been her shadow since she was a toddler. Whatever Diana did, Tia wanted to do. Being too young to be accepted for training as a potential Wall Archer, she had talked her Aunt Arti into helping out on the archery range after school and chores.

"Did you get a chance to shoot today?" Tee asked.

"Yes," gushed Tia. "I used Diana's short bow and got two arrows in the red."

"Practice pays off, Tia," said Tee with a smile.

"It's not my bow, Tia, I told you it's yours," said Diana.

Tia beamed.

As they walked back toward town, Ansen pulled him off to the side and said, "Tee, you need to watch Angus. I don't trust him. I've seen him intentionally hurt people while sparring. He covers it well, but I can tell it's not an accident. He definitely has it out for you for some reason, and I wouldn't put anything past him." Tee nodded in agreement. This wasn't news to him. But it was significant that Ansen was so concerned.

Pacifica

CHAPTER 4

SCHOOL PROJECT

Emily Clarkson walked to the front of the room. She was young and enthusiastic. As she leaned forward to start her lecture, it was apparent she enjoyed what she was doing.

"Good morning," she said, smiling. "We will complete our study of Pacifica emigration history by examining the moral questions that resulted in our planet being divided between true humans and GEMs. As you know, our people ventured far from Earth and into another galaxy to escape the brutal Mutant Wars. While GEMs, Genetically Engineered Modifieds, are different from us, we consider them to be human. We were determined to avoid taking part in the genocide of those considered non-human. "Our people hold the belief that we need to keep humankind free from genetic engineering. We do not believe we have the knowledge to predict all the impacts that might result from editing our genome or epigenome. If history has shown us anything, it's that playing God has unintended consequences. While we are firmly against genetically altering humans, we do not believe we have the right to exterminate other humans just because they have been altered.

"This moral stance has come at a high cost. The GEM race was designed to be aggressive, thrive in hot and cold environments, and have a high reproduction rate. These attributes seem reasonable as advantages to surviving across the many challenging environments of Pacifica. Implementing this genetic engineering had serious unintended consequences. We do not believe the designers intended their progeny to lose most, if not all, of their empathy. We believe this loss of empathy is what enabled the development of a culture that glorifies subjugation and brutality.

"In short, GEMs are a race of psychopaths. There seems to be something innate in their makeup that causes them to enjoy the pain and suffering of others. They appear to have no remorse. The very worst of human traits. As our enemy, their selfishness and desire for individual dominance is a weakness, since it interferes with their ability for large-scale coordination.

"Our ancestor's view was that genetic engineering was not necessary for survival on this planet as long as we restricted colonization to the coastal, mountainous areas. Our peninsula is perfectly placed for us to thrive. It is much milder than the majority of the continent. Even given that restriction, we knew our people would have to evolve to be stronger and more resilient.

"This is a difficult planet for humans to thrive on compared to our home planet of Earth. We know we are larger and stronger than the original colonists based on the few surviving medical records from that period. While we avoided genetic engineering, there was a mandated breeding program in place for roughly fifty generations. This was a dark period in our history where some men and women were not allowed to have children. Others were forced to conceive with multiple people who were selected based on their physical attributes.

"You can imagine raising children with your wife that had come from a variety of donors. Or a wife not allowed to have children but having to accept that her husband was being used as a donor to impregnate a variety of women. Somehow, traditional marriage survived. But it survived by placing an extremely high emotional cost on those who had to live through it.

"The desire to be allowed to have children with your spouse explains in large part why there is still a strong cultural bias toward visible robustness. People were driven to marry those who were viewed as desirable breeding stock. Logically, this shouldn't matter anymore. We have evolved and we thrive. Evolution no longer needs to be directed or encouraged by social norms.

"Your assignment, due a week from today, is to select one of two topics. For either topic, write an essay describing the moral dilemma and why colonists made the decision they did. Summarize agreement or disagreement with those decisions with clearly worded arguments.

"Choice number one. Knowing what we know now, should we have gone against our moral stance of not eliminating the GEM race when we had the chance? Are there situations when genocide is a good and moral choice? Does it matter whether genocide is carried out on true humans or genetically enhanced humans?

"Choice number two. Should we have resisted mandatory breeding programs? Should we have had faith that evolution would naturally occur? Would we have a heathier society today if different decisions had been made? What should we do, if anything, to adjust the cultural bias toward size and strength resulting from this?

"When I have reviewed and graded all the papers, I will select a few contrasting opinions, and we'll have a debate."

"This afternoon we have a special guest," Tee's teacher continued. "In the back of the room is Professor Delvin Dacy, who is Dean of Landfall University." Heads turned around. "His specialty is technology and engineering with an emphasis on antiquities. He was involved with the design of our Tram and will give a lecture on that topic after school for those who are interested. He also chairs the admittance board for university applicants. He will be observing for the next two days and will interview those of you interested in the university. He is also well informed on technician training schools in Landfall City and is available to answer any questions you might have."

Tee wasn't surprised. Everyone knew the professor had come to see his next-door neighbors Quinn and Hestie. They would definitely be offered admittance to the university. Both were scary smart. Everyone said they were the best students coming out of Apple Valley in a generation.

For most, a decision for vocational schooling or an apprenticeship was worked out with parents. For families who owned a business, a child's apprenticeship was simply moving full time into the family business. For a rare few, a position at the mysterious university was offered.

Quinn was one of his best friends. He supposed they were friends because they were both a little odd. Quinn's oddity was his incredible intelligence coupled with an incurable good nature. Quinn was always happy and positive, no matter what was going on. He assumed the best in everyone, even when there was ample evidence to the contrary. He seemed to have an inability to recognize evil intentions. Unlike Quinn, Hestie was reflective, shy, and quiet. A deep thinker. She had an uncanny ability to read people. Diana and Hestie were best friends, so the four of them hung out a lot together at school.

Tee was daydreaming. It was always a negative mark on his school evaluations. Every year it was the same thing "Tee needs to stay engaged in class," "Tee is intelligent but lacks focus," etc., etc., etc. He was mentally planning his next hunting trip when Diana suddenly shot him a glance, looking horrified.

Turning to look at Hestie, she seemed concerned as well. Tee shook himself and re-played what had been going on in class. They had moved from history to math. Angus had been asked a simple math question related to fruit farming weights and measures. He was unable to answer. No surprise there. Pear farming was his family's business.

But Angus was not very bright. He was large, athletic, extremely bad tempered, and quick to imagine insults. In short, he was a bully. If there was a shared goal at school, it was to avoid Angus getting angry. Everyone except Quinn understood the right thing to do in this situation. Hope the teacher didn't call on you, and if she did, struggle to answer. Or even better, give a wrong answer.

However, Quinn, as usual, head in the clouds, didn't understand the danger. He probably answered quickly because the professor was observing. Quinn's only goal in life was to go to Landfall University and study engineering. Angus had turned bright red when Quinn correctly answered the question. Diana's and Hestie's horrified looks said it all.

When recess was called, the teacher asked Quinn and Hestie to stay behind. Tee relaxed. If Quinn missed the first recess, maybe a confrontation in the schoolyard could be avoided. Knowing Angus, Tee knew something would happen, eventually. Oh well, hopefully that could wait for another day.

CHAPTER 5

RECESS

Griff was well hidden in the brush wearing his camouflage cape and waiting for recess. The school was on the edge of the woods, so it was a simple matter to get close. The boys and girls separated into various groups, some talking and a few boys sparing. Everyone was avoiding being near or even looking at the large, brooding boy with an angry expression on his face. He guessed this was Angus. The region VC who had recommended the boy had said, "He has a few personality quirks and a quick temper."

Physical contests between the boys were encouraged. The constant war with the GEMs meant they needed to be prepared. It was normal for boys to agree to spar at recess as long as no hard punches were thrown.

Sometimes surreptitious surveillance was a waste of time, and it looked like this was one of those times. Then a heavy-set sort of nerdy looking boy walked out. He had a big grin and greeted one of the groups. The angry boy, he had guessed was Angus, walked over and, with no warning, punched him. The nerdy kid was still smiling when Angus's fist hit him square in the jaw, knocking him to the ground. Angus then started kicking with obvious intent to cause damage as the downed boy rolled into a fetal ball.

Griff was getting ready to rise when a short and slender boy stepped up and said, "He's yielded Angus."

"Stay out of this turd," replied Angus, and kicked hard again.

The smaller boy jumped forward and pushed Angus away, then backed up and said, "Leave him alone, Angus. If you want to fight someone, fight me."

Well, thought Griff, this is interesting. Bravery is one thing, but this kid has a death wish. Just then, the small boy darted in, landed an ineffectual punch, and darted out again. Well, at least he's quick, thought Griff. Angus lost his temper, abandoned his training, and threw a wild punch, which the smaller boy ducked. The small boy then stepped in and tried to take Angus out with an uppercut. He missed. After that, it got ugly really fast, since the smaller boy was now inside Angus's reach.

Griff got himself ready to rise once more as Del and the teacher walked out. They quickly broke up the beating, well it wasn't really a fight anymore. As Griff settled back down, the smaller boy looked directly at him with anger and accusation written all over his face. Even more interesting, thought Griff.

CHAPTER 6

VOLUNTEER COMMANDER

Major Richards greeted Griff with a firm handshake and said, "Griff, it's been too long. Don't see a lot of the Guard up here. Gets a bit lonely in the wilderness."

"When does your rotation end, Major?" Griff responded.

"One more year, then someone else gets to look after these yokels. I will admit they are a sturdy bunch, and their reputation for honesty and decency is understated. They've made me feel at home. So much so, I've given some thought of retiring here."

Major Richards was the Apple Valley Volunteer Commander, or VC. He was still a vigorous-looking man, but the years showed. Richards looked noticeably more tired than the last time Griff had seen him. It might be time to find Richards something less demanding than region VC when this year was up. These assignments were typically given to older respected Guard officers as the first stage of retirement.

Every man, woman, and child in the region was in a volunteer unit. These units had their own officers, non-com's, logistics, and support staff. The VC was in charge. His duties included a full understanding of the capabilities of the region and being on the lookout for potential Guard recruits. If the unit was called to the

Wall, the VC reported into Commander General of the Guard, or CGG.

"I heard you might have a recruit for us," Griff offered.

"Yeah, his name is Angus, and he's a brute," Richards replied. "You may or may not remember his father, Asher Willard. He was a recruit twenty years ago but didn't make the final cut. Evidently Asher didn't take his failure well. He's been obsessively training that boy and his younger brothers ever since they could walk. Wants them to accomplish what he himself could not.

"Angus's fighting skills are excellent. His flaws are that he's a bit dimwitted, loses his temper easily, and tends to underestimate his opponents. This has been encouraged by the fact the competition up here isn't what it is in the lower valleys. When he does lose, it's usually because he gets impatient and is out maneuvered." Richards hesitated, then said, "The other thing is a tendency to over dominate. Once we get him out from under his father's influence, I think these traits can be ironed out."

"As you know, I've been here for a couple of days," Griff said. "First day, I covertly observed the schoolyard during recess. I saw all the flaws you mentioned during a fight he initiated with another boy in the yard."

"Let me guess," said Richards. "Was it Tee Stone?"

"Yes, how did you know that?" asked Griff, surprised.

"Tee won a bout against Angus a couple of weeks ago and it embarrassed and infuriated him," Richards replied.

"Let me guess, he outmaneuvered him," Griff said with a smile and they both laughed.

"I think it did Angus some good to realize every enemy is dangerous. However, it is troubling that he doesn't accept his fault in this. He tells the others Tee cheated. As you know, there is no such thing as cheating in a fight," Richards said, smiling.

"But given the faults, your recommendation is that we invite him to recruit training?" Griff asked.

"Yes, his potential is too good to pass on. We need to fix the flaws."

"Tell me more about Tee," Griff said.

Richards was surprised. He hesitated as he thought it over and then responded, "To be honest, I wish he weren't so small. He's a tough nut, I can tell you that! He rarely wins hand-to-hand matches, but he never gives up. It isn't lack of practice, skill, or effort. Everyone eventually realizes they just need to overpower him. That is when he doesn't trick them into doing something stupid. Which he does more often than you would think. I've often thought the perfect warrior would be a combination of his cousin Ansen's athleticism and Tee's smarts and toughness. Ansen has the physical skills but doesn't have the drive, motivation, and ruthlessness necessary to make it in the Guard.

"He's a natural leader. Tee was picked the past two years to lead Apple Valley's capture-the-flag team. Another reason why Angus might resent him. During those two years, Apple Valley has won every match. The consensus of the other regions is that 'Tee is a tricky bastard.'

"In the tournament this year, he won in the early rounds by employing multiple probes designed to evaluate his opponent's decision processes and biases. These resulted in some sophisticated envelopment maneuvers both offensive and defensive in nature. They get worn down by losing lots of little battles until he's stripped a strategic portion of their defense. Then he goes in for the kill. He somehow convinces his opponents they know what he is up to. They don't.

"In the final he bunched his team in the center, stripped his own defenses, and gambled it all on a mass charge right up the middle. His opponent was Landfall City. He knew the quality of that team was far above his. Leaving your flag naked is not a recommended strategy, but it worked.

"The reason it worked is he had gotten everyone to expect a defensive posture with multiple light probes. His standard war of attrition. He started by probing the middle in every previous engagement. So they didn't take the initial attack seriously until it was too late. Outside of his leadership capabilities, he's an excellent runner and has unusual skill in swimming and archery. He can actually swim all the way across Apple Lake, bizarre, huh? While nobody can touch Arti, he comes closer than anyone else to beating his mother."

Griff paled. "Tee is Arti's son?" he asked.

"Yeah, can't you see the similarities?" Richards replied.

In a flash, Griff realized that Tee's slender frame was similar to his mother's with facial features suggesting a family connection. Griff was stunned, but hoped it didn't show. He was embarrassed to admit, even to himself, that he was obsessed with Arti.

It had started years ago. He was below the Wall with a squad. They were outflanked, overwhelmed, and in danger of being decimated. Arti had shown up and quickly cut down enough of them for the squad to retreat back to the Wall. How she had placed arrows between Guard members on the move was incredible. More impressive was her choice of targets. She understood the flow of the battle and strategically cut down just the right GEMs to open up a path for retreat while protecting their flanks. The combination was awe-inspiring.

Once they reached the Wall, he realized his Newbie hadn't retreated to plan. He had veered down the Wall and was now separated from his squad. Wading back into the fray with his squad along the Wall, cursing loudly as he went, he was surprised to see he still had archery support. An archer should not have an angle along the Wall for this.

Looking up, he couldn't believe what he saw. Still starkly vivid in his memory was Arti standing exposed on the top of the Wall instead of safe behind a crenation. She stood tall against a clear blue sky like an angry goddess. Tall but unusually slender, her red hair was tied back but flowing with the wind as she dealt death one arrow at a time. She saved his life. She saved the whole squad. He was thunderstruck.

Thanking her for what she had done later, he discovered that while she was intense, she was also surprisingly warm. Still angry, he had marched the Newbie up to her to apologize for his idiocy. She couldn't have been more gracious. She actually thanked the Newbie for "protecting all of us."

And with that, Griff was lost. Asking around he found out she was married. He then firmly tamped down his attraction, but retained his admiration for her courage. Now the fantasy came rushing back.

"Griff, are you okay?" Richards asked with concern.

"Yeah, sorry, what did you say?" Griff replied.

"I said, Tee is on my list for volunteer officers' training. He isn't meant for work below the Wall. But he certainly has potential to provide leadership and decision making on and behind the Wall. When he graduates this spring, I'll let him know and start his training."

They spent the next hour discussing the overall defensive capabilities and logistical status for the upper lakes area. At the end of the discussion, Griff asked, "Are the volunteers on the cliff top lookout posts staying diligent?"

Richards reddened and replied with embarrassment, "To be honest, I haven't hiked up for an inspection in a while."

The upper valleys were remote mountainous areas with their outer boundaries jutting out of the ocean. The cliffs were sheer and high, with large waves crashing into them. However, the GEMs were smart, aggressive, and persistent even in the face of overwhelming challenges. Twelve Guard posts had been strategically set up high in the cliffs to look for boats and directly observe the few beaches that might allow a team to land and scale the cliffs. It was windy, cold, and utterly boring. But it had to be done. So, two men per Guard station were always in place. Surprise inspections were needed to keep the volunteers diligent.

"Probably a good idea to go scare the hell out of them," Griff suggested. He could tell Richards was not looking forward to the strenuous hike. It will be good to rotate him out next year, Griff thought.

As he walked back to the inn, he scolded himself for his juvenal obsession. The Guard was a small elite group that stuck together. So much so that Guard member families were a close-knit community, spending considerable time together at Guard events. It was an extended family. If he proposed Tee for recruit training, and he somehow made it, there would be events where he would interact with Arti. "I can't let this craziness interfere with making the right decision on Tee. God help me get ahold of myself," he prayed.

CHAPTER 7

FRIDAY NIGHT BONFIRE

Starting in spring and throughout the summer and early fall, Tee and his friends built a bonfire on the beach every Friday evening. Those were magical evenings. Laughing, eating, joking, telling stories, playing games, and just being young. Others would come and go, but the core group of five would always show up.

Tonight, Tee was sitting off to the side and watching. School would be over next month, and the world would change. This didn't seem to be bothering anyone else. Hestie was shaking with laughter, listening to Ansen tell one of his ridiculous stories. They had heard all his stories many times. That didn't seem to make them any less funny.

Ansen could make anyone laugh, even the ever-serious Hestie. Diana was on the other side of the fire, smiling and faking interest in whatever Quinn was trying to explain to her. It was likely incomprehensible. Quinn was always animated, happy, and enthusiastic about whatever his latest interest was. He made you want to be interested, even when you had no idea what he was talking about.

The five of them had been together forever, it seemed. Uncle Hugh, Ansen's father, had stepped into a parental role when Tee's father had died. He treated Tee like a son and included him in all family events, great and small. A year older, Ansen was more like a brother than a cousin. While Ansen had a biting wit, he also had a big heart and took on the role of protective big brother. Quinn and Hestie lived next door.

Their mothers were good friends and, as children, they wandered back and forth constantly between the two houses. He could always count on Quinn for a smile and Hestie for deep, serious conversations. She always pointed out the best in everyone. Both had been good and loyal friends to the slender and short oddity they lived next to. Not that the twins were any less odd. Tee could remember thinking he was stupid until he realized everyone was stupid compared to the twins.

Finally, Diana. Tee fondly remembered the first time he met Diana. He had been told two days before that his father had died at the Wall. He was in his second year in school, so he must have been six. All the kids knew what had happened and were avoiding him. Apple Lake was a small community.

During recess, Tee was sitting by himself under a large oak tree when a small voice said, "I'm sorry about your dad. My dad says he's a hero." Tee looked up to see a pale face framed by long soft hazel colored hair. Her blue eyes were shining with unformed tears and her lower lip was quivering. Tee's mother had not yet come back from the Wall. Tee was terrified she might be dead, too. Diana's compassion broke the emotional dyke he had been defending.

Tears started to silently stream down as he turned his head away. Diana sat down, reached out, and put her hand on his. She didn't say anything, just sat with him as he quickly got his tears under control. Tee was very embarrassed. Warriors don't cry. If any of the kids found out, he would be humiliated. Diana never said a word about it. Not to him. Or anyone else. Ever.

Hestie and Diana were fast friends. A few weeks later, Diana found out from Hestie that Tee's mother was Arti. "Is Arti really your mother?" Diana had asked, her eyes wide. Tee shook his head yes and Diana continued. "My mom was classmates with her and says she's really nice." Tee beamed. Most people only seemed to care that his mother was a famous archer. They didn't realize what a great mom she was. "Can I meet her?" Diana asked quietly.

"Sure," said Tee. With Diana's mother's approval, Tee brought her home and proudly introduced his friend Diana.

Arti smiled and asked, "How is your mother? I haven't seen her in a while."

Diana replied. "She's fine. She says to send me home if I pester you too much."

"Pester me? Whatever about?" Arti replied with warmth.

"Well, I like archery. She's worried I will bother you asking too many questions," Diana responded with a worried expression on her face.

Arti laughed loudly and said, "Archery questions never bother me." Arti looked at them both with a smile, thought a minute, then said, "Tee goes most evenings with me and shoots at special targets while the Archers practice. He has an extra bow that would be right for you; would you like to join us tonight?"

Diana's blue eyes grew impossibly larger, and she said breathlessly, "Yes, I would love that." Diana had been a part of his and his mother's lives ever since.

Ansen suddenly called out, "Hey, Tee, what are you doing over there in the dark? I thought I told you to only do that in private." They all laughed. Tee blushed and was glad it was dark. Ansen could say things nobody else could get away with. If Tee or Quinn had said the same exact thing, it would have come across as creepy.

"Sorry Ansen, just thinking. I understand your confusion, since you don't know how to do that." A good comeback that got a few smiles. You had to fight back carefully with Ansen. The last thing you wanted was an insult competition because you would lose.

"Come over and warm up by the fire, Tee," Hestie said. If anyone understood the need to just sit and think, it was Hestie. Tee walked over and plopped down next to her and Ansen. Guessing what troubled Tee, she asked, "What are you going to do after school lets out?" It was a little spooky how Hestie seemed to know what people were thinking and feeling.

Tee shrugged and said, "I'm not sure."

"We need help in the blacksmith shop. Dad keeps giving you hints, Tee," Ansen chimed in.

"I know, but Pete is perfect for that and almost ready. I don't want to be in his way," Tee said with a sigh.

"Knock it off, Tee," Ansen said angrily, "You are part of the family; didn't we all make that clear years ago? You have just as much right to join the family business as my brother does."

"I didn't mean it that way," Tee replied. "I'm just not as interested in blacksmithing as Pete is." He hesitated a moment and then said, "I talked to the professor today after the Tram presentation. There is a mechanics training program down in Landfall City. Ever since they put in the Tram, I've been interested in machinery. The sawmills and food processing plants running off the Apple River above and below the falls are fascinating. Maybe we can find a way to expand the blacksmithing business into machinery. I just need to figure out how to afford the school."

Tee then looked at Hestie and asked, "How did your interview with the professor go, Hestie?"

"Good. He's nice, in a gruff sort of way. He told Quinn and I that he will be putting both our names forward for admittance. He's pushing Quinn toward the engineering department but wants to know more about what I'm interested in."

"From what little I understood about what Quinn was saying earlier, I don't think he has to push him very hard," Diana said, smiling as she looked warmly over at Quinn.

Quinn had just opened his mouth when Ansen jumped in with a plea, "Diana, please don't get him going again."

Quinn smiled and said, "Okay, okay, no more trying to educate Luddites tonight."

"I would ask what a Luddite is, but I really don't want to know," Ansen said.

"So, what are you interested in, Hestie?" Tee asked.

"I'm not sure. I know I want to help people. Becoming a doctor sounds interesting, but I'm not sure what kind. Pediatrics and psychiatry both seem interesting."

Ansen smiled devilishly and said, "So little kids or crazy people."

"Well, knowing more about both might help me understand you a little better, Ansen," Hestie said with a rare jibe, causing everyone to laugh.

Tee sat back, completely at ease. Life couldn't get any better. He wished it could stay this way forever.

CHAPTER 8

DINNER AT THE INN

Del sat in the dining area of the bar at the Apple Lakes Inn waiting for Griff to arrive. His back was stiff. His legs ached from the hike up the falls. He had been walking gingerly since he had arrived. I really need to get more exercise, he thought.

Growing up in Apple Valley, he had gone up and down the falls trail more times than he could count. It seemed so easy when he was a young man. It was especially galling how cheerful Griff had been when they reached the top. Pointing out how perfect the weather was for hiking and with a sweep of his arm pointing out the tremendous view from the top. Griff wasn't normally this cheerful and Del knew it was his way of poking fun at Del's state of fitness.

He knew it was ridiculous to compare himself to a professional soldier. Especially one who thrived on exercise. But it was galling all the same. If he was fair, Griff had suggested stopping and resting several times. He knew it wasn't because Griff needed it. Anyone else from the Guard would have been trying to walk him into his grave.

Although Griff had a gruesome reputation within the Guard, he hid a dark secret. The man was, in reality, a bit of a softy. That is, if he respected you. He was especially polite with women.

Neither of them were married. In his case, he simply didn't have time for a wife. Academics was what he lived for. He had an occasional woman friend from time to time. But more often than not, it was someone he was collaborating with. It was lonely sometimes, but he had accepted many years ago that he would be a lifelong bachelor.

Del didn't know why Griff had never married. That wasn't a topic anyone was brave enough to bring up with him. Griff actually seemed to be a bit afraid of women. Which was somewhat endearing in such a gruff and violent man. Del certainly wouldn't tell anyone he suspected Griff had a soft side; he wasn't stupid. But it did cause him to smile.

Griff walked into the inn, sat down heavily, and without any pleasantries said with a grimace, "Do you have real beer up here? Or is the fruity crap all there is?"

"Good evening to you, too. As for the beer, you'll just have to tough it out, Griff," Del said with a smile. Before the Tram, it wasn't reasonable to cart much up the falls, even alcohol. At this point, there was pride in being different." Del moved a bit closer and whispered, "Not that you care, but the locals heard what you said and are smirking." Griff just rolled his eyes and shrugged.

Del ordered peach whiskey. When it arrived, Griff tasted it tentatively, made a sour face, and exhaled with a loud sigh, shaking his head in disgust.

"The good news is fresh venison is available tonight if we order quickly. Some local hunter just brought it in," Del said.

"It won't make up for the crappy drinks, but that is good news," Griff said with a sour grin. He then turned serious and said, "What do you know about Tee Stone?"

Del's face scrunched up in surprise and he said, "Strange you ask about him. In a normal year, I would be putting him forward. He's no genius, but his leadership potential is unusual. Strong enough academically, but with skills in mediation and negotiation beyond his age. He has a knack for organizing and collaborating. His teacher says everyone likes him."

"I know of at least one person who doesn't," Griff said, smiling, and they both chuckled, remembering the fight, or more accurately, the beating.

Del continued, "There are a pair of twins that are special, truly special. I will get them both admitted. I'm from this region so it will look preferential proposing two candidates. I can make that work by calling in a few favors. Once the other professors get Quinn and Hestie into class, any questions about preference will disappear. However, I can't make three work, no matter how well deserved."

"So, he's less irritating that your typical university know-it-all." Griff scoffed.

Del hesitated as his eyebrows came together. Then he smiled slowly and said, "I guess that's the truth of it. You have to admit the Guard has more than its share of overly large egos."

Griff smiled back at him and said, "You realize we are likely the worst of them." They both laughed.

"So why ask about Tee? He definitely doesn't look like Guard material," Del observed.

Griff chuckled. Shaking his head, he sighed and looked out the window with a troubled expression. Then he said, "He's unusual." Griff paused and sipped his whiskey, then said, "When I'm evaluating someone for the Guard, I sneak close to the exercise yard on the first day to observe how they interact with the other boys. Aggressiveness, ruthlessness, and a desire to win at all costs are Guard virtues. But so is teamwork. Bullies make poor additions to the Guard. They can be useful below the Wall but more often than not create more problems than benefits."

Griff took a deep breath and continued. "You saw the end of the fight at recess," Griff said. "First, it wasn't Tee's fight. He was protecting another kid who got sucker punched and was being viciously beaten. Having the smallest boy out there trying to break it up was weird. That it clearly didn't surprise any of his classmates made it even weirder. Second, instead of delaying for the teacher to come out, he pushed him hard, causing him to lose his temper and swing wildly. It was obvious he expected this, as he avoided the punch. Then he stepped inside for the kill. It was very aggressive. As you saw, the result wasn't pretty. His counterpunch had to be perfect, and it wasn't. That's when you walked out."

"I was horrified to see how badly beaten Quinn was," Del said.

Griff sighed and said, "So, that's one of your geniuses. Good thing he's smart because he's useless in a fight. If Tee hadn't stepped in, I would have. Given that he did, I decided to see what would happen." Griff smiled. "I expected him to get his ass kicked. And he did. What really shocked me was the realization he knew I was watching the whole time. When the teacher broke up the fight, he looked directly at me. He held his stare just long enough for it to be an accusation. I'm guessing he thought I should have stepped in. When I didn't, he made a snap decision to defend. Maybe to force me out of hiding. I was really well hidden and camouflaged. He should not have noticed me. That level of awareness in someone who hasn't been trained is unheard of."

Griff took another sip of his whiskey and continued. "To make it even more interesting, I had a recruitment meeting with the Apple Valley commander. He immediately started campaigning for Angus. No surprise there. Was quite effusive about it. Described him as skilled, tough, and highly motivated. He did observe that Angus was 'overenthusiastic in dominating others,' Guard speak for bully. He thought teamwork might be a problem, but thought he was worth a try.

"Then I asked about Tee. He was surprised at first. Then he said he wished Tee were bigger. He had the toughness, motivation, and instincts to join the Guard but clearly didn't pass the eye test. What really interested me was his success in the regional capture-the-flag games. As you know, that game mirrors aspects of military strategy, and he seems to be some kind of savant."

"Okay, so Tee has traits you like. You can't seriously be thinking of him as a recruit," Del said with surprise.

Griff sighed again and said, "Warfare isn't one dimensional. The most successful scouts are not always the best fighters. The best scouts seem to be those with endurance, awareness, patience, but most of all, judgement. Being a good officer is all about judgement and an ability to get others to follow you. As you know, our selection criteria are focused on hand-to-hand fighting skills and the ability to survive below the Wall. This is critical, but not sufficient, in my opinion."

Del held up his hand and said, "Hold on, I've met Dee. He would chew someone like Tee up and spit him out the first day. And the CGG would be applauding while he did it."

"Probably, yes," Griff replied with another troubled

sigh.

"Tell me more about your geniuses. What makes them so special?" Griff asked.

"They're twins. A boy and a girl. Their father was an engineering student of mine years ago. Someone I collaborated with on the Tram design. He's a smart guy, easygoing, a bit odd, but does good work. Not a standout. Their mother Dorothy is another story. She is a once in a generation intellect. She was recruited and groomed to join the university staff as a researcher. Her mentor thought she would end up as chair of the university's medical research department someday.

"They're both from Apple Lake. Childhood sweethearts. They wanted to move back. She is one of the local doctors but consults with the university on a regular basis. She gets asked to help researchers filter out complexities to help in identifying cause and effect in their research data. She has an amazing and unique ability to see information in massive and confusing data sets."

Del paused to take a sip of whiskey. "Hestie is gifted, but perhaps not as unique as her mother. What is different is she has an abundance of empathy; reading people and situations extremely well. As you know, it's not unusual for really smart people to have limited social intelligence. Her mother, for instance, has a reputation for making blunt observations she doesn't realize are quite insulting. Hestie has the potential to be an excellent medical research doctor working directly with patients. Will be interesting to see what she eventually decides to do with all that.

"Quinn is brilliant and passionate about technology and engineering. The projects he showed me in his rickety workshop are far ahead of anything I've seen in a student entering the university. He has been engaged in an extensive self-study of topics that interest him since he was able to read. He will likely jump ahead at least a couple of years right away. I'm already convinced he will make enormous contributions. The challenge is that Hestie seems to have gotten all the social skills their parents had to give. It's entertaining to watch the two of them interact with others.

"They're extremely close and both well-liked by those who know them. Hestie for obvious reasons, but Quinn because he is always in a good mood bubbling over with happiness and enthusiasm about whatever has caught his fancy. Hestie artfully sooths over the bruised feelings Quinn creates for those who don't know him, while their friends just accept that Quinn is Quinn."

"Not sure I've seen you this enthusiastic about university candidates before," Griff observed.

"We'll we've had several whiskeys which might explain part of my enthusiasm."

"You've had several whiskeys; I could only stomach the one," Griff said with a sour look and a shudder. "I'm going to stay a few extra days. I want to do a little more background on Angus and talk with him. It turns out they have a capture-the-flag scrimmage this weekend. I want to observe and maybe talk to Tee a bit too. I may deliver recruit invites if I'm convinced they deserve them. I expect you're heading back tomorrow."

"Yeah, I'll be away before breakfast, so I'll see you at the next planning session," Del said.

Griff stood up from the table and as he walked away, he turned and said with a sarcastic grin, "Enjoy the Tram ride down."

Del just waved Griff away, smiling. *I will definitely enjoy the ride down,* he thought. *I probably revealed* more enthusiasm than I should have. I am wildly excited. But unfortunately, I can't reveal why my friend.

"Barmaid, one more whiskey please," Griff requested. After it arrived, he continued to sit, privately delighted, sipping his drink slowly, and making plans.

CHAPTER 9

INVITATION

Griff could hear the yelling before he rounded the corner and could see the farmhouse. He was surrounded by a pear orchard, so decided it must be the Willard farm. The house and the orchard didn't look well maintained. Most farmers were diligent with their crops and farming equipment. Some less so with their houses, but most kept things clean and orderly. This farm was neither.

Standing in front of the barn was a tall, broad, overweight, red-faced, scruffy looking man about Griff's age flailing a young boy's bare bottom with a belt. He was screaming, "You worthless piece of shit! You're not worth the food I give you."

The boy had his pants down around his ankles, blood dripping down one leg, and tears streaming down. His mother just stood there watching. Terror evident on her face. Angus and two other boys were standing in the background. Angus was showing a very thin smile, as if he might be enjoying this.

They all suddenly spied Griff approaching. The man stopped beating the boy and in a challenging voice said, "Who are you and what do you want?" Before Griff could answer, he added, "Whoever you are, I don't like strangers on my property, so state your business and then get the hell out of here."

Griff continued to walk up without responding until he came face to face with him. "My name is Griffith Ricks. I'm Master Sergeant for the Guard. I'm here to talk to Angus on Guard business."

The man looked surprised, and now perhaps a bit embarrassed. How he could be surprised that Griff was in the Guard given he was in uniform was hard to understand. He held the blood splattered belt in one hand while gripping the boy with the other. Now that Griff was closer, it was obvious he was drunk. His breath and clothes reeked of alcohol. His features firmed up and he shoved the boy to the ground and said sternly, "Get back to work." Then, looking back at Griff, he said, "You talk to me about the Guard, not Angus."

Griff's face froze, he stared him down, and then calmly said, "You must be Asher Willard."

"Yeah, he's my boy, and he does what I tell him to do. You here to invite him to recruit training?" Asher said, glaring back.

"Angus has reached his maturity and doesn't need your permission for anything anymore," Griff said. "I'm happy to explain Guard recruit training with parents once an invite has been given so they can advise. I'll come back after I've talked to Angus to answer any questions." Griff then turned to Angus and said, "Come take a walk with me."

Asher Willard's brows crashed together. He opened his mouth as if he would object but then turned and while walking away yelled, "Woman, get me a whisky."

Griff walked back down the path away from the farm and said, "Angus, I would like to invite you to Guard recruit training. The next session starts in two weeks."

"Thank you, sir. I was expecting an invite. I think I'll

like being in the Guard," Angus said without a shred of humility.

"You'll have to get through training to get into the Guard, and it's going to be difficult. We don't take everyone we invite," Griff said.

"The only thing I'm worried about is whether some current Guard's kid gets pushed ahead of me. I deserve to be in the Guard, just like my dad deserved it. Everyone knows getting in isn't all about merit," Angus said in a challenging voice.

Griff stopped, turned to Angus with a frown, and said, "I always encourage recruit invites to say or ask anything in the initial conversation. If that was a question, let me assure you merit is the only criteria for entry into the Guard. If that is an accusation, be very careful who you voice it to in the future. Guard members, including myself, don't take kindly to false accusations." This was delivered as an obvious threat.

Angus leaned forward with a look on his face as if to argue, thought better of it, and said, "I accept the invitation. I just want to make sure recruit training is fair."

Griff was watching Angus carefully. This kid was a volcano ready to erupt. After seeing the heartbreaking scene in the yard, he could understand why Angus might have some issues. He hoped the thin smile he saw on Angus's face was a nervous one and not enjoyment. It had taken every shred of control Griff had not to thrash the father. He would report the boy's abuse to the local sheriff when he got back to town. He would strongly recommend the sheriff make sure the woman was okay. He was especially worried about her.

"One other thing, Angus," Griff said, reverting to his

calm voice. "There are two invites this year for recruit training."

"So, you invited Ansen?" Angus said with a tinge of a sneer.

"No, I'm going to invite his cousin Tee," Griff said in a bland voice.

"What! You're kidding me," Angus said, laughing. "No way that little turd is qualified for the Guard."

Griff's face clouded as he started to get angry again, told himself to calm down, and said in a stern voice, "I decide who's qualified for an invite, not you. I know there have been some issues between you and Tee. That stops now. Guard members are brothers from the moment they are invited. You will put away any ill feelings toward him now or turn down the invite. He's going to be told the same thing."

Griff watched Angus as he looked to the ground, obviously trying to control his anger. Angus took a big breath, let it out slowly, and looked back up. Griff stared him in the eyes for a few moments and said, "Are you accepting the invite to recruit training?"

Angus looked down again and said in a flat voice, "Yes, sir."

With that, Griff turned around, and they walked back to the farmhouse. Asher Willard was sitting on the porch drinking from one glass while another was sitting on the table beside him. He said, "We got started on the wrong foot. Sit down and have a drink."

"No thank you. I don't drink in the middle of the day," Griff said, not willing to pretend this was going to be a cordial conversation. "Your wife should join us so she can ask questions, too."

"She's too stupid to have anything worth listening to.

Making dinner, cleaning the house, and warming my bed are the only uses I have for her," he said, chuckling as if Griff would get the joke.

He didn't. "Any questions?" Griff asked curtly.

"No, I know everything about the Guard. I want to hear you promise Angus won't get cheated out of a spot in the Guard like I was," Asher said in a challenging voice.

"Our selection process is based on merit. Those who don't get in are simply those who don't measure up. Any other questions?" Griff said in a tense voice.

"No," Asher said, fuming.

As Griff walked around the bend in the road, the loud and angry voice of Asher Willard could be heard again. Evidently, Angus had told his father that Tee had been invited. He couldn't make out all the words, but scrawny and turd came through clearly. Then he heard Asher say in a clear voice that Arti must have spread her legs to get Tee an invite.

Griff stopped, gritted his teeth, and took a deep breath. He stood there stiffly for almost a minute until his anger was under control and then walked on. He knew what he would do if he went back. He decided the best thing was to pretend he didn't hear it and move on. Was Richards right? Griff wondered. Could they really fix Angus by taking him away from his father? Could they instill Guard values? He didn't have a good feeling about it.

After giving a report to the Sheriff, Griff asked where he could find Tee. "He's likely up at the archery range. Practices all the time," the sheriff reported and then said, "Thanks for the information on Asher. We are constantly going out there to resolve problems with neighbors and making up excuses to check in on Sara and the kids. Sara won't say anything bad about her husband and makes up stories to cover her and the kid's injuries. 'I walked into a door, he fell down the stairs,' etc. She's terrified of him. I know somebody is eventually going to get seriously hurt. But I can't do anything until they do."

Griff was nervous about the next stop. He hadn't spoken with Arti since her heroics at the Wall those many years ago. But first he had to go find Tee and make the invitation. Deciding to invite Tee had been a hard decision. The easy part was the leadership, intelligence, creativity, and boldness he exhibited in Apple Valley's capture-the-flag games. It was a child's game, but it showed attributes he thought were sorely needed in the Guard.

By itself, it wouldn't have been enough. Griff had to be confident an invitee could get through recruit training. Tee's immediate defense of his friend on the playground was what ultimately swayed him. The boy had courage. He was willing to fight a losing battle. He just didn't have the size the Guard was looking for.

Griff walked into the clearing and saw Tee with a very pretty, tall, and athletic looking girl. They were shooting arrows at a distant target with impressive accuracy. Griff stopped and watched for a while, finally deciding Richards wasn't exaggerating Tee's expertise with a bow. The girl was getting all her arrows inside the red circle, but spaced somewhat randomly. Tee's were all grouped dead center. He guessed having Arti as a mother probably had something to do with that.

He walked up and interrupted them saying, "Excuse me, Tee, do you have a few minutes?"

Tee and the girl turned around, both surprised to see him there. "Yes, sir. Diana, I'll be back in a few minutes."

He gave her a quick smile, turned around, and walked off with Griff to a bench just out of earshot.

"Are you here to ask questions about Ansen?" Tee said.

"No son. I actually here to offer you an invite to Guard recruit training."

Tee's mouth opened, shut, opened again and with a shocked look on his face he sputtered, "You have to be kidding me."

"To be honest, if you accept, everyone is going to think it's a joke of some kind," Griff said in a quiet voice.

"But I'm way too small to be in the Guard," Tee said.

"Everybody has deficiencies. As far as I can tell, this is your only significant one," Griff said seriously.

Tee stopped and looked down at the ground. He started to say something, stopped, and thought some more. Finally, he said, "Thank you for the offer, sir. I don't know what to say. I never imagined anything like this. Can I talk to my mom and think about it before I give you an answer?"

"Of course. I'll need to have your decision by this time next week since I'll make someone else an offer if you refuse," Griff said kindly. He thought it was a good sign that Tee wanted to think it over.

"Ansen would be a much better choice for this," Tee said.

Griff's face softened, then he said in a soothing voice, "These discussions we have before you accept or reject my offer are completely private. Anything you say will be kept in confidence, never to be shared with anyone. Can you promise the same before I comment on Ansen or tell you about the challenges you'll face if you accept?"

"Yes, sir, I will keep what is said between us," Tee said in a serious tone.

"Your cousin has a lot of good qualities. He's an exceptional athlete, but just an excellent fighter. He's not exceptional because he doesn't have the drive and passion to persevere, no matter what. This isn't a bad quality in a person. It's completely normal. But normal is a bad quality for a Guard recruit. If he was going to be invited, it would have happened last year when he graduated," Griff said.

"I understand," was all Tee had to say.

"I've invited you because the Guard needs to expand its capabilities. All our lives are at stake. Fighting it out below the Wall is a vital part of our defense, but it isn't adequate. You've shown great skill in discovering weaknesses in your opponents and creatively taking advantage of them. While capture-the-flag is a child's game, you've shown exceptional leadership, planning, and execution in those contests these past two years. I think those skills translate to the future of the Guard.

"Unfortunately, you are small in stature and that is going to cause you a lot of suffering if you accept my offer. Fortunately, you are large in heart, incredibly large, it seems. You'll need all of it because it won't be easy, and it won't be fair. If I thought you might quit once you start, I would never make an invite to you," Griff explained. Then he waited patiently for Tee's reply.

Tee thought some more, looked up and with fire in his eyes said, "I have been bullied my entire life. I know recruit training would be far worse than anything I've overcome. But, If I can make a difference to keep my family and everyone else safe, then I don't see how I could do anything other than say yes and see it out until the end."

Any doubts Griff had vanished. He was right about Tee. Recruit training was going to be extra ugly. But this is what a leader in the Guard should look like.

"A little background, in case you don't know this already. Recruit training consists of forty-five days of shake out, or as we call it IH, In Hell. A large number of those invited quit voluntarily during this. It is brutal, degrading, and only the very strong survive. Next, we have ninety days of combat training with an emphasis on learning to fight as a team known as AH, After Hell. Some drop out in this phase. Usually because they realize they won't make the cut.

"We limit graduation to the top fifty recruits based on a point system you can learn about later. After that, we spend another ninety days on basic training that assesses each recruit for various training regiments that will last for another year to eighteen months. Everyone is extensively trained for fighting below the Wall. But some are given extra training, such as scouting or development for promotion into the officer ranks.

"However, remember, everyone is a fighter first. Talk it over with your mom and let me know your decision, Tee," Griff said, smiling. He then handed him a piece of paper and said, "Here is where you can reach me. Get your decision to me by this time next week. Now, how do I find your mother so I can answer her questions?"

"She's down at my aunt's below the falls, and it's not clear when she'll return. My aunt has been really sick, and Mom is taking care of her and my cousins," Tee said.

A huge weight came off of Griff, and disappointment quickly replaced it. He was embarrassed that Arti had such an impact on him. It was ridiculous at his age. He didn't even really know her, for heaven's sake. He shook off his jumbled thoughts and said to Tee, "Give her the address and I'll try and answer any questions she has. Given she's spent so much time at the Wall, and much of that supporting the Guard, she probably has a good idea what you're getting into."

Griff's face took on a softer appearance, and he said, "Some advice if you're open to it. You'll learn in the Guard that you never reveal strengths or weaknesses to an enemy. You are going to have to think of the instructors and the other recruits as enemies until graduation. Your bunkmate being the only exception. With that in mind, keep your swimming ability a secret. Letting it be known will just offer another avenue for abuse."

Tee certainly understood that one, he thought. His most recent nickname was a perfect example.

"Last item. The other invite from Apple Valley was given to Angus Willard. I know there is history and you two don't get along. The minute you accept the invitation, Angus is to be viewed as a brother. That means you have to let all the history go. Do you understand?"

"I understand and I will do that," Tee said.

Griff was pleased. He was a little surprised that he had been harboring more doubts than he realized. Those doubts had been erased. Now he concentrated on how he was going to win the initial fight with Nate and Dee. Nate was the CGG, Commander General of the Guard, and Dee was the head drill instructor. He knew both of them really well, having served together in various capacities. He knew they would hate Tee on sight. Griff relished a good fight. Especially one with no rules.

CHAPTER 10

OBLIGATION

Tee told Diana about the invite as soon as Griff left the archery range. He guessed he should have kept it a secret so he could be sure to be the one to tell his mom. 'That bird has flown,' as Grammy liked to say. Diana had given him a strange look when he first told her. She seemed sad instead of the mixture of excitement and worry he had expected. Then she continued the oddness by saying how much she *and* Ansen would miss him if he accepted. How proud *they* would both be.

Diana had never spoken of her and Ansen like that before. She always spoke in terms of herself and let Ansen speak for himself. It was strange and perhaps a subtle message that she perceived his interest and was letting him know it would lead nowhere. That certainly made it easier to consider leaving Apple Valley for good. Guard members spent the bulk of their time near the Wall or at the numerous ocean cliff side forts. It stung, but it was also the type of thoughtful, caring gesture Diana would make.

His mother heard about the invite almost immediately, of course. She asked him to come down the falls and stay with her at his aunts for a few days. His aunt lived with her husband and his other cousins just outside Apple Falls. Tee didn't know these cousins as well. They lived below the falls, and they were much younger. His aunt was the youngest of Grammy's children and much younger than his mom and uncle.

Arti gave her son a big hug and pulled him into the chaos of a home with four children ranging in age from six months to four years. Tee had been an only child but was used to the hum of activity from the time he spent at Uncle Hugh's with his Aunt Anny, Ansen, Pete, and Tia. It was a familiar and welcome feeling.

"So how long was it going to be before you told me?" Arti asked with hands on hips and a stern expression.

"It's only been one day, Mom," Tee replied. "I should have kept it private until I got down here."

Arti's eyes softened and then she said, "I'm very proud of you, Tee."

"Thanks, Mom, but I don't know if I'm really cut out for the Guard," Tee replied.

"The Guard doesn't offer invitations to recruit training unless they're certain you are," Arti said firmly.

"Their master sergeant who invited me claims I have capabilities the Guard lacks. He told me it would be especially hard for me as the instructors and other recruits would resent someone of my stature getting invited," Tee said with a questioning face.

Arti's face softened again, and she said, "I am slender and have lived with the jibes and offhand remarks my whole life. One of the reasons I have worked so hard on my archery was a desire to feel better about myself. Your father was short. You got the worst of that combination. Your father was also very smart, loving, and charismatic. I'd like to think you got the best from both of us instead of the worst."

Arti hesitated, then continued. "Regardless of your blessings and challenges, you've been asked to sacrifice.

To make a difference for your family and all of Pacifica. Your Friday night bonfires only happen because of the sacrifices made by your father and countless others." Arti stopped and waited for Tee to respond.

"Grammy says protecting others isn't a choice, it's an obligation," Tee said.

"My mother is a wise woman. She lost two sons and a son-in-law at the Wall but has never wavered," Arti said softly.

"To be honest, I don't have questions about whether I should do this or not. Guess I've spent too much time with you and Grammy for that," he said with a sad grin. "I just want to make sure you're okay with it."

"I won't lie and tell you I'm not worried. But I would be disappointed if you chose not to accept this invitation. All our lives depend on being able to defend our little piece of heaven. The Guard has recognized that you are a special young man. Embrace it, Tee."

CHAPTER 11

CELEBRATION

The plan was to get together Friday night at the beach for a sendoff for Hestie, Quinn, and Tee. Then Grammy declared she was showing up. If Grammy was showing up, then everyone from all four families would be there. Grammy had been a big part of all their lives. Babysitting, entertaining them with stories, telling fortunes with her deck of cards, and occasionally applying consequences for their youthful indiscretions. She had this head thumping thing she did. She would flick her middle finger hard alongside your head. It stung, but didn't actually cause any damage. They had all gotten head thumped at some point, even Hestie.

Ansen joked that he had a permanent indentation on the side of his head from the number of times she got him. You had to be on the lookout for her if you had done something wrong. She also provided an ear for anything and everything. You could tell Grammy your deepest secrets and know they would remain private. Of course, you were required to receive her 'good advice' in return. It was advice you might not want to hear. But you knew the advice was good even when you chose to ignore it. Although not related, Hestie was eerily similar to Grammy in that regard.

Years ago, Tee had told Hestie, "Grammy is who you'll be in sixty years." He'd meant it as a joke.

Hestie hesitated, looked at him seriously, then her face slowly transformed into a shy smile. "That might be the best compliment I've ever had. Thank you Tee."

He had been taken aback by her reply. Older now, he was starting to really see and appreciate Grammy. It really was a nice compliment. Tee sat down next to his grandmother on the rough bench he and Ansen built for her years ago. "Why did you come down to the beach tonight, Grammy?"

Grammy looked at him with a sparkle in her eyes and said, "There are important events in life, Tee. You ought not to miss them. I've known all of you since you were babies. You are as important to me as you are to each other. Sorry I'm invading your bonfire, but I wanted to enjoy it with all of you. Don't worry, I'll go early and leave you young people to your fun. Just humor an old woman for a couple of hours."

Tee raised his hands palms up, shook his head side to side and said, "Grammy, don't be silly. You're welcome to stay as long as you want. I'm glad you decided to 'Invade.' It's fun having everyone here. Much better than our typical Friday. Maybe we should have been doing this all along."

"Nonsense. Young people should get away from old people and have a little fun," she said with a warm smile. She lowered her voice. "Are you nervous about recruit training Tee? Before you answer, you should know I won't accept lies from you tonight," Grammy said with a fake stern look on her face.

Tee loved that his grandmother could be blunt and empathetic all at once. It was quite a skill. "Yes, very, but don't tell anyone," he whispered with a smile.

Grammy smiled back nodding and said, "Your secret

is safe with me. What worries you?"

"The Guard recruiter told me I would have an especially hard time. He said there will be instructors at the school offended I was offered a slot in recruit training and will try and get me to quit."

"We were all surprised when you were chosen. Not because you don't deserve it, but the Guard does seem to have its standard look," Grammy said thoughtfully. "You can do this Tee. You've been pig-headed, stubborn, and prone to single-mindedness since the day you were born. You don't give up even when you should. So, I pity those who try to get you to quit."

"Well, thanks for the compliment, I think," Tee said, smiling warmly. "Quitting isn't what I worry about. I'm worried that however hard I try, I still won't make it."

"If you give it everything you've got, and don't make it, we'll all be proud. Especially your mother," Grammy said confidently. "I'm not worried about that, and you shouldn't be either." She searched his face until she was satisfied he had really heard her and then said, "One last question. Are you going to tell Diana how you feel?" Grammy asked with softness in her eyes and voice.

"No, she doesn't need that, and neither does Ansen. If I tell her, it will be uncomfortable forever between the three of us. She loves Ansen, and he loves her. That's the end of it." Tee wasn't sure how Grammy had extracted his feelings for Diana from him. She had a way of getting people to tell her things they hardly admitted to themselves. At the time, it had felt good to tell her, but she needed to stop harassing him about that.

"Okay, Tee, I will stop. For now, anyway," Grammy said with a wicked smile. "I do need to tell you this. We ALL believe in you. Remember that when it gets tough.

Now, go, have fun with your friends. This time next week you'll be on an exciting adventure. Be sure to enjoy it, especially the tough times."

Grammy watched Tee walk back toward the fire and his friends with love and sadness swelling in her breast. She would miss him, Hestie, and Quinn terribly. They would never know how much she would miss not having them nearby. The three of them needed to move on with their lives and I need to support that, she thought. Just think of how Tony and Dorothy must feel. Both their children are moving away at the same time. At least she would still have Ansen and Diana nearby. She loved her grandsons fiercely, and Diana was a wonderful girl. She would be thrilled to have her in the family. Shaking her head, she marveled over how blind and stupid young people were. Diana and Hestie love each other and all three boys. Tee and Ansen are more like brothers than cousins. But none of them seem to have a clue about what's really going on. I'm glad I'm an old woman and don't have to live through the stupidity, pain, and suffering of being young.

As the fire died down, Grammy decided the young people had had enough of old people for the evening. She gave Anny 'the look' and Tee's aunt said, "Pete, Tia, let's go, it's time."

"I want to stay. It's Friday night. No school tomorrow," Tia said, pouting dramatically.

Tee's aunt hesitated. Everyone knew that Ansen and Diana would stay at the fire after everyone else had gone. This had been their pattern all spring. It would interfere with their blossoming romance if Ansen had to walk Tia home.

"Tia's no bother Aunt Anny. If you let her stay, I'll walk her home," Tee said. He had a special place in his heart for Tia. It was impossible to be unhappy around her. Tia was responsible for everyone calling him Tee. She had had trouble pronouncing his name as a toddler and when she started reading, she noticed their names started with the same letter. "Everyone says his name wrong. It should start like mine does," she said. Then she started just calling him Tee. It stuck.

His aunt looked at Tee warmly and with a smile said, "Okay, we'll have a little peace in the house this evening. Make sure it's not too late."

Tia ran over, jumped into his lap, and gave him a huge hug, "Thank you, Tee!"

"No problem, squirt," he said, smiling with a warm glow inside. Tia was always so endearingly dramatic with her affections.

"I want to stay too, Mom," Pete said with a slight whine for effect.

"If Tee walks you home with Tia, then fine. In the meantime, you listen to Ansen. When he says it's time to go home, you go. Do not overstay your welcome. If you give Ansen any trouble, you'll have your father to answer to," his mother said with a stern look on her face and his father nodding in the background.

"Okay, Mom," Pete promised, while showing a little frustration in his voice. Pete was a mirror image of Ansen halfway through his final growth spurt. He would grow to be as large or larger and was already quite the athlete for his age.

Instead of having Ansen's easygoing nature, he was intense and focused. He thought he was old enough to walk Tia home. Just like he thought he should already be working in the family blacksmithing business. Tee was his latest hero in getting an invitation to Guard recruit training. This was something he hoped to do someday, and so he peppered Tee with questions.

"How long is your training? When will you know you've made it? Do recruits really die during training? Will they send you to the Wall? Can you send letters telling us how it's going? Can I send you a letter? Why did you get an invitation and Ansen didn't?" This last question was an obvious dig at his older brother, and Pete had glanced sideways at his brother when he said it.

"Whoa Pete, one question at a time," Tee said, laughing. "I'll send letters to your Aunt Arti, and she'll read them to everyone. You can send me letters too. But I won't receive or be able to write letters for forty-five days. They call that In Hell, the first part of the Shake Out. I know training is intense, but I'm pretty sure they aren't trying to kill us. I don't know much about the Wall other than your Aunt Arti's stories. The Guard is secretive about their training, so can't answer questions because I don't know."

"Pete, give it a break. You've been after him all night. As far as why he was selected, it's pretty simple. Tee is the toughest dude you'll ever meet, and he's really smart about warfare stuff. I am neither of those things." Then, with just the right hesitation, he added, "I am, however, much better looking," Ansen said while glancing over at Tee with a smile. Everyone groaned.

Ansen's self-awareness and self-confidence were amazing to Tee. Ansen knew what he was, and he knew what he wasn't. His little brother's insult was quickly shrugged off with a joke. What had become an uncomfortable situation became comfortable again. Not that Ansen wouldn't get even with Pete, that would come later. Pete was destined to suffer from a barrage of not so good-natured ribbing when Ansen decided it was time for payback. Pete really ought to know better.

"What made you write the 'little people' essay, Tee?" Diana asked, with mirth dancing in her eyes. I've never seen Ms. Clarkson so frustrated. The best part was when she chose you to debate your 'opinions' against Hestie, who made exactly the opposite arguments."

"That was fun," said Hestie, smiling. "I do think you pushed it a bit too far in the debate by suggesting genocide against little people to free up resources might have been the morally correct decision. You were supposed to pick one topic after all."

Tee, smiling with an evil grin, said, "I don't know. She looked right at me as she was describing the effects of negative cultural biases against those of small stature. It was the sympathetic part of the look that did it. I actually got a really good grade. She said irony combined with sarcasm and humor are an effective means for getting people to think. To question their belief systems. She told me that after her initial shock, she decided Hestie and I had coordinated our papers and the debate as a political protest. As you know, she is all about the downtrodden. She said I ought to consider a career in social work or politics. I laughed all the way home."

"That was probably the most fun I had in class all year. Everybody talked about it for days," Diana said, her eyes bright.

The chatter continued until Tee was sitting with Pete, Quinn, and Hestie, watching the fire as it burned its way down to the embers. He looked over to where Ansen, Diana, and Tia were sitting and could tell it was time to call it a night. Tia was entertaining Diana, as only Tia could do. But the look on Ansen's face said he had had enough of his sister's theatrics for the evening. "Well guys, I think it's time for me to go," Tee said.

"No!" said Tia. "It's still early and I won't see you before you leave."

"I promise to come by the house before I leave, Tia," Tee said.

"Pete, Tia, it's time to go. Tee agreed to walk you home, and it's time," Ansen said with a firm look going back and forth between them.

"Hestie and I will go with you guys," Quinn said, getting up and perhaps showing one of his rare instances of social awareness.

So, the five of them headed down the path toward Apple Lake, with Pete barraging Tee once more with questions as Tia glued herself to Hestie, chattering like a bird. Quinn brought up the rear, deep in thought. Tee had snuck a quick look as they left the clearing. He saw Ansen and Diana leaning their heads together and fought down his rising jealousy. I really need to get a grip, he thought. He was lucky to have Ansen as his cousin. And lucky to have a lifelong friend in Diana. He would get past this. They would all be friends forever. He just needed to keep reminding himself.

As he was sorting through his emotions, he heard the menacing voice of Angus say, "I told you your cousin wouldn't always be around, turd." Tee stopped as Angus and his two younger brothers stepped out onto the trail.

"We're supposed to put the past behind us, Angus. We're brothers now, remember?" Tee said with steel in his voice.

Angus stepped forward and said, "I kick the shit out of my brothers all the time. Why should you be any different?"

"I don't want to fight, Angus," Tee said firmly.

"You don't have a choice, turd," Angus said as he

rushed forward, diving toward Tee's knees. He was intending to get him on the ground to negate Tee's quickness. Tee knew once he was on the ground, he was lost. He had seen Angus employ this tactic before, and in an instant, he stepped forward and planted his knee directly into Angus's nose with a loud crunch.

Angus held both hands to his nose, swearing as the blood rushed out and said, "You're dead, turd."

Tee backed up to give himself more room. He had noticed out of the corner of his eye that Tia had kept her head. When Ansen and his brothers showed themselves, she immediately ran back toward the beach to get Ansen. If he could delay long enough for Ansen to show up, this would turn into a fair fight. He knew Angus would likely back away at that point.

Tee didn't notice that Angus's youngest brother had gotten behind him. So, when he shuffled backward, he unknowingly backed right into him. He got pushed forward, right into Angus's arms.

Tee was forced to the ground, and Angus started beating him viciously. Chaos erupted. Hestie was screaming for everyone to stop. Both Quinn and Pete had jumped in to help but were pulled off Angus and into separate fights by the brothers. Quinn was quickly knocked to the ground by Angus's youngest brother, who pummeled him as he lay curled up on the ground. Pete was faring better, fighting off the older of the two brothers when Ansen slammed into Angus, knocking him off Tee. The two of them stood up and squared off.

"This isn't your fight, Ansen," said Angus, sounding like he had a cold from the blood in his nose.

"It is now, asshole," Ansen replied as he surged forward with a series of punches, driving Angus backward. After a hard punch to the stomach, Angus dropped his guard, and Ansen nailed his broken nose with a hard left jab. That dropped Angus to the ground where he stayed, holding his nose and swearing. All the fight had gone out of him.

Hestie touched Tee's shoulder lightly and asked, "Are you okay, Tee? You got hit pretty hard in the head." Then Diana came over to examine him as well and they both started treating him like a toddler who had just skinned his knee. Tee didn't know which was worse. Getting beaten up by Angus or getting sympathy and ministering from Hestie and Diana.

He had never felt so humiliated. Why did anyone think he could become a member of the Guard?

CHAPTER 12

ANGUS

Griff arrived in Apple Valley early in the morning. He was very grumpy. He had been riding a horse or hiking most of the day before and all night. He had gotten an urgent message from Richards the morning before that Tee had been ambushed by Angus and his brothers and was injured. By sheer luck, he had been up toward the north end of Eureka Valley, which made a quick trip possible. No sleep, but possible. The week before the start of each recruit class was very busy for Griff. He was not happy to start it off this way.

Griff's main concern was whether Tee was so injured he couldn't start training. Missing a cycle would mean his invitation to Tee might be discovered and that would make it harder to force him through. Unless Richards was misrepresenting what happened, his next task was to tell Angus his invitation was being revoked. He was sure that was going to be an interesting conversation, especially with Angus's father.

Griff knocked on Tee's door and a badly bruised Tee answered the door. "Good morning sir, would you like to come in?" Tee asked with deference.

"Are you okay, son?" Griff asked with obvious concern.

"Yeah, just a few bruises. I'll be fine," Tee answered back while limping slightly into the front room of the home. Sitting in the front room was an old woman with bright, warm eyes. Tee motioned toward her and said, "This is my grandmother."

"Pleased to meet you, ma'am," Griff said.

"Mr. Ricks is Master Sergeant for the Guard, Grammy," Tee said to complete the introductions.

"So, you're the one who invited Tee to attend recruit training," Grammy said, locking eyes with Griff.

"Yes, ma'am," was all Griff said.

"Good, you're polite. You must also be smart if you understand Tee's worth," Grammy said and gave him a devilish smile.

"I'm not sure about the smart part, ma'am. But I am impressed enough to want him in the Guard," Griff said respectfully. He hesitated while Grammy continued to examine him and then said, "Tee, can we talk somewhere privately?"

Grammy stood up and walked toward the door. She hesitated with her hand on the doorknob and said, "I'll head out. Time to get home and feed the animals. Tee you stop by later, okay?"

"I will Grammy. Love you," Tee said.

"Love you too, my boy," Grammy said as she closed the door behind her.

"I need to hear your version of what happened, Tee," Griff said.

"It's pretty simple. Angus attacked me while I was walking home from our regular Friday night bonfire. I had my two younger cousins with me, as well as my next-door neighbors, Hestie and Quinn. He stepped out of the dark and told me he wanted to fight. I reminded him of what you said. I told him I didn't want to fight. Then he attacked me," Tee explained.

"I've heard he has a badly broken nose," Griff said questioningly.

"I kneed him in the nose when he dove at my legs. Tia ran to get Ansen, who showed up pretty soon after the fight started. He pulled Angus off me and hit him in the nose again. It did look pretty bad," Tee said.

Griff stared at him for a while and then said, "I believe you."

"Just like that?" Tee asked.

"Just like that," Griff confirmed. "Will you have any trouble making it to training?"

"I can make it to training, but am wondering if I'm really who the Guard needs," Tee said. "My cousin Ansen had to save me. I'm doubting whether I can make a difference."

"You can make a difference," Griff said firmly.

Tee hesitated, took a deep breath, and said, "Well then, the choice is easy. Grammy was just here repeating what my mom said. If you can make a difference, then it isn't a choice, it's an obligation." And then Tee visibly relaxed and with one corner of his mouth raised, said, "Recruit training can't be worse than having to face Grammy if I fail to make good on an obligation." Tee then turned serious and said, "I will treat Angus as my brother in the Guard. I'm sorry things spun out of control."

Griff relaxed inside. This just confirmed once again that he had made the right decision.

"Okay, we'll expect you next week. Do not be late," Griff said with steely eyes. "Is your mother back yet?"

"No, my aunt is still sick but getting better. It's going

to be another day or two. She said she really doesn't have any questions. Just wants to make sure I recognize and honor my obligations," Tee said.

As Griff left Tee's home, he was angry. Really angry. He knew he should have calmed down before he went out to the Willard farm. But he was on a mission. As Griff rounded the bend and saw the farmhouse, he could see that Asher Willard was on the porch drinking again. And early in the morning too. He took a deep breath to calm himself and walked up without announcing himself.

"What are you doing back here?" Willard said. "Guard training doesn't start until next week and Angus has work to do until then."

"Where is Angus? I need to talk with him," Griff said.

"You can tell me whatever it is he needs to know," Asher Willard said. Just then, Angus came out of the barn, stopped, and then casually approached the two of them.

"Angus, I'm here to tell you not to bother coming to Guard training next week," Griff said sternly. "Your invitation has been revoked. I told you to treat Tee as a brother and yet you decided to ambush him. And you couldn't even do that by yourself. You had to have help."

"That's not what happened," Angus shouted back. "Ansen, Pete, and Tee ambushed us while we were walking home."

"So, you're a liar as well as a coward," Griff said firmly.

"Don't you call my boy a liar. Real men scare you, don't they? You don't want them in your precious Guard. I've had enough of you wimpy Guard bastards. It's time you get your ass kicked by a real man," Asher said as he stepped forward.

Mrs. Willard took one step toward him meekly, put her hand lightly on his chest and said to her husband, "Let's just calm down and talk this over."

Asher's face exploded with anger. He backhanded his wife, sending her head over heels off the porch, and charged Griff.

He thought later that the backhand was what did it. Usually, he would have simply restrained someone in this situation until they calmed down. Especially someone drunk, out of shape, and no threat to actually hurt him. Instead, Asher was being tended to by the local doctor for a broken sternum. He had hit him with enough force that it looked like Asher would likely have a permanent deformity from it.

Angus had stepped in to help his dad and gotten his nose broken again for his troubles. Griff actually felt a bit bad about that. It was sort of mean. What bothered Griff more were the sobs coming from Sara Willard. He couldn't imagine what her life must be like living in this household.

The incident cost Griff the rest of the day. A day he could ill afford. The sheriff had to get testimony from him and all the witnesses at the farm. If Griff had not been Master Sergeant of the Guard. And if the Sheriff hadn't already been looking for reasons to lock Asher up, he might have been held longer. Hope for the family arrived in the form of Dr. Dorothy Espers.

Griff was impressed with the local doctor's no-nonsense approach. She insisted that all members of the family undergo a medical evaluation. When she finished the examinations, she presented the Sheriff with her written opinion that the wife and youngest son were being subjected to life-threatening physical abuse. She recommended they get the judge to issue a restraining order and move Sara Willard and her youngest son to a safe location. They ended up spending some time that afternoon talking about medical procedures at the Wall and what could be done to improve them.

Griff realized he had met her before, but in the heat of battle, he really hadn't paid her much attention. He took a mental note to set up some time with her and the Guard medic corps to discuss some of the improvements she suggested.

As the sun was setting, Griff reached the bottom of the lower falls. Another hour and he would be at the Apple Falls Inn. Two whole days and one night wasted.

CHAPTER 13

IN HELL

It was a cold, brisk, clear day and Dee was in an extremely good mood. He was nearly forty years old with dark hair, icy blue eyes, and a bulldog face. With massive arms and legs, his strength was legendary. His fighting skills were second only to Master Sergeant Ricks. He was bundled up against the cold with his heavy parka. Steam was coming out with every breath.

He always looked forward to training up the future of the Guard. Dee was short for "Drill Instructor." A nickname given to him years ago. He embraced this assignment so much that he encouraged its use. By now, everyone had forgotten what his real name was.

In Dee's mind, there was no contribution higher than taking boys with raw ability and turning them into Guard Newbies. He was pleased and honored that he was the one who owned this critical function. Dee gladly dedicated his life to making the Guard better.

IH was always interesting. You learned who was mentally tough, and who wasn't. It was always surprising who stood out and who quit early. The Hell part was a bit misleading because the physical fitness and depravity portion of training was done at a training facility in a high valley. It was cold at any time of the year. The elevation mixed with the cold was a challenge all by itself. They would move to their main training facility down below the Landfall Dam once this portion was complete. This allowed for better skills training and taught them to deal with the heat as well.

He expected this was going to be a special group. Not all recruit classes were equal. Some were weaker, and some were stronger. This class had a lot of Guard members' sons. It wasn't nepotism. In fact, the bar was a bit higher for them as nobody wanted to be embarrassed. Growing up, they understood what life in the Guard was all about. They also had a parent who was an elite warrior helping them perfect their fighting skills. He was especially enthusiastic that Barin Phillips's son Jay was in this class. He had watched him win the youth hand to hand combat championship the previous spring.

In his opinion, Jay was a unique talent. Likely better than his father, and that was saying something. Not that he would let any of them think they were better than pond scum. You had to knock them down before you could build them up. He smiled, thinking about the shock some of the city boys would feel being cold all day long. They were used to warm buildings and thick coats in this type of weather.

As he walked toward them, standing at attention, he saw a short, skinny kid with lots of bruises. He had to look twice because he couldn't believe his eyes.

Dee marched up to him and said, "What the hell are you doing?"

The boy hesitated, then said, "I was told to report here, sir."

"By who?" Dee asked, glaring at him.

"Master Sergeant Ricks, sir," Tee answered.

"For what?" Dee shouted.

Tee hesitated again, looking confused. Then he finally

said, "For Guard training, sir."

"What's your name son?"

"Theron Stone sir. But most people call me Tee."

"I don't care what people call you. Wait here," ordered Dee.

With that, he turned away from the muster and walked away without an explanation. The quartermaster who had mustered them saw one head turn to look, and he marched over and screamed in the offender's face, "You are at attention! You will not move until Drill Instructor Dee tells you otherwise, understood?"

"Yes, sir," the recruit barked out in a nervous voice.

"I don't have time for this nonsense. What is Griff trying to pull?" Dee said as he walked purposely away from the muster, "It's got to be a practical joke. The kid is short, skinny, and looks like a good stiff breeze would take him away."

He first went and found Sergeant Derick, his physical fitness instructor. "Why do we have some kid who clearly can't pass your entrance test in my muster this morning?"

"He passed all the tests, Dee. I know it's weird, but he's actually in exceptional physical condition. Minus the bruises, of course. Came in first by a large margin on the ten-mile run. Wasn't even breathing heavy at the end. One third of the recruits were bent over, gasping for breath as soon as they crossed the finish line. The big city boys are used to a lower elevation, but that's no excuse. We'll need to run them hard for a few weeks."

"Where did the kid get the bruises?"

"One of the boys from his hometown beat him up last week. Heard the other kid didn't get hurt at all," Derick said with a sneer.

"Oh, for God's sake. So, he couldn't even fight off some random hick?"

Dee walked toward the officers building, fuming. When he got there, he knocked hard three times on the CGG's door.

"Who is it?" the CGG asked.

"Dee sir."

"Enter." While he was walking through the door, the CGG said with irritation in his voice, "What do you want, Dee?"

"A midget showed up to report for training, sir. Says his name is Theron Stone," Dee said.

"So, reject him as unfit," the CGG said.

"He's passed the physical fitness entrance exam and Griff is the one who gave him the invite," Dee replied.

The CGG breathed out hard, dipped his head in frustration, snapped it back up, and barked out, "Corporal! Go find Master Sergeant Ricks and tell him to report here immediately."

"Yes, sir," came the reply.

After enough time had passed for them both to recognize that Griff didn't report immediately, he opened the door without knocking and casually walked in with a smile, "Good to see you Dee, it's been a while."

"You can't seriously be proposing some undersized kid for the Guard," said the CGG, looking at him sternly.

"He's not a typical recruit, sir. He has skills and potential in areas the other recruits do not have. The Guard needs to broaden its capabilities," Griff said firmly.

"Dee has rejected him for not passing the entrance

test," the CGG said.

Griff looked over at Dee in surprise and asked, "What test did he fail?"

"The eye test," Dee said.

Griff hesitated and then said with a frown, "You can't reject him because you don't like the way he looks. If that were a test, you wouldn't be in the Guard either."

"Very funny, Griff. What are you trying to do? Make a mockery of us all?" Dee continued angrily. "He got the crap kicked out of him just last week. From what I heard; the other kid came out of it without a scratch. Recruits ought to at least be able to defend themselves from the local yokels. They are supposed to be the best of the best."

"That local yokel was originally invited to recruit training. He ambushed Tee with his brothers due to some imagined past insult. He knew they were both headed for Guard training. I told both of them to bury any animosity and treat each other like brothers. I withdrew his invitation because we don't need that type of kid in the Guard," Griff said with conviction.

Then, in a frustrated tone, Griff said, "I'm trying to get both of you to realize that hand to hand combat is not the only tool we should be utilizing against the GEMs. I understand every recruit needs to be effective below the Wall. Size and strength are not the only weapons that can be deployed."

Griff hesitated a few moments and then said, "By the way, Dee, you should at least get your story straight. The other kid has a badly broken nose and won't look quite the same going forward."

As Griff swung his head back toward the CGG, Dee shrugged, stepped back, and leaned against the door with his massive arms crossed. He smiled as the CGG and Griff argued back and forth. CGG said that the integrity of the Guard was at stake. Griff went on and on about the benefits of offensive and defensive diversity in battle. He knew Griff would win. He was the CGG's first sergeant years ago and CGG idolized Griff almost as much as everyone else did. Even if he did yell at him a lot.

Dee reflected on the time when the CGG as a Newbie had wandered away from Griff's squad during a retreat at the Wall. Griff immediately ordered them all back out there to save him. When they finally returned to the safety of the Wall, the volume, variety, and duration of Griff's obscenities had been a thing of beauty. Griff even made the CGG go apologize to a Wall Archer who had helped them.

The truth was that Griff would be the CGG today if he had wanted it. And if that had happened, Dee would probably be master sergeant. It was frustrating, but he knew he wasn't in Griff's league. Nobody was. On the other hand, he honestly thought he made a bigger contribution as a drill instructor than any other job the Guard might assign him to.

So, in the end, it was what the Guard needed. And that was all that mattered. Having admiration for Griff didn't mean he wouldn't enjoy watching Griff fail with one of his crazy experiments. Especially one Dee felt threatened the integrity of the Guard.

As Griff continued to bludgeon the CGG, Dee could see the end was near. He appreciated the CGG standing up to Griff. Most of the officers did everything but salute when Griff 'suggested' a course of action. While it was good to see a fighting man making the life and death decisions on the battlefield, this was wrong. That skinny kid had no business being considered for the Guard.

"Okay, Griff, enough," the CGG said, ending the debate. "Dee, start him with the others, but let me know when he quits," the CGG said, looking back to Griff with a challenging smile.

"Yes, sir," snapped Dee. Then he pivoted around and walked out.

After the door was closed, Griff said with a cold stare, "Nate. You know he's going to do everything he can to run the kid out of training."

"Good, the sooner the better. If a miracle happens and he gets through training, I'll buy you a drink at the graduation ceremony," Nate said with an even bigger smile. "If not, you'll owe me a drink and Dee a drink and an apology."

As Dee walked back to the muster, he wondered how to best orchestrate a quick exit. The recruits had been standing in the cold at attention in their light exercise garb this whole time. He could see some of them shivering. He knew they were jealous of his thick parka. Does them good, he thought. The city kids had no idea of how severe the elements could be. How the cold could suck the strength and willpower out of a man. They would learn quickly, or they would be gone. "At ease," he ordered and picked up the clipboard he had been looking at when he first noticed Tee.

A sudden thought hit him. *Why don't I assign Jay Phillips as Tee's bunkmate?* As the son of a solid Guard member and winner of the youth combat competition, he was entering the Shake Out with very high expectations. Jay was taller than most, with a physique even Dee was jealous of. Handsome with red hair, blue eyes, and light skin blushed red by the sun. Hyper competitive with a reputation for ruthlessness in the fighting ring. Dee thought Jay would be extremely pissed off getting an albatross as a bunkmate. He'll help me push him out, thought Dee, smiling inside.

Of course, he couldn't smile on the outside. That would lead recruits to the conclusion he was human and not the devil himself fresh from hell to torture them. He would make the next forty-five days hell on earth for these recruits. Then the work would begin.

"Pay attention. I'm not going to repeat myself," Dee barked out. "Most of you are not good enough for my Guard. The sooner you leave, the better. Better for you, better for the Guard. I've seen poor recruiting classes before. This has to be the worst. One out of five failed to meet the physical fitness entrance exam yesterday. They are gone. The entrance exam was a warmup. It was easy. Going forward, it's going to be hard. Anyone ready to quit?"

Dee stared at them and then locked his icy glare onto Tee, letting him know he wasn't wanted. "So, I guess this recruiting class is not only physically weak, it's filled with morons," Dee said, continuing his cold stare at Tee.

"We only allow fifty recruits into the Guard with each recruiting cycle. That means that more than half of you will not graduate. I don't believe there are fifty in this class worthy of the Guard. If all of you quit, and we have nobody in this cycle, I will have done the Guard a service. If we have more than fifty left at the end of training. The top fifty recruits based on points awarded will be admitted."

"The Guard relies on teamwork. We all win, or we all fail. You will be assigned a bunkmate who will stay the same until one of you quits. When that happens, a new bunkmate will be assigned from those that are left. You will eat, shower, and shit at the same time as your bunkmate. They will be your partner in all things. Points are awarded individually or as bunkmates, depending on the exercise. You cannot make the top fifty if you haven't accumulated a large number of bunkmate points. If you have bad teamwork, if you have a bad bunkmate, you won't make it."

"Quartermaster will announce the bunkmates list. When your name has been called, go with your bunkmate to the barracks and pick out your bunk bed. This will be your home until you quit. Next, go to the quartermaster. He will provide you with uniforms, bedding, and supplies for personal hygiene. Quartermaster will then muster you all back out here so we can get to work."

Dee then stepped back and let the quartermaster call out the list. He had instructed him to leave Jay and Tee until the end. That way, he could watch the tension slowly grow into horror as Jay realized Tee might be his bunkmate. It also meant they would get the worst bunk bed available. Dee had to fight to keep the smile off his face as the second to last bunkmates were named. The look on Jay's face was priceless. Frustration, fear, and anger all mixed together. This was going to be fun.

The first few days, Tee felt like he was actually in hell. Then it got worse. They were up before dawn and still at it until well after dusk. Sometimes they were rousted out of bed after an hour or two of sleep for an all-night march. One time, they were awakened in the middle of the night to wade quietly up a stream for hours through freezing water, learning to 'hide their movements.' They had twelve recruits quit during that exercise, to the delight of the instructors.

Tee thought his normal, heavy exercise routine would help. It didn't matter. The instructors knew your weaknesses and were brutal in exploiting them. Jay, his bunkmate, was a machine. He was strong as a bull and quick as a cat. A natural athlete with excellent endurance. He was the ideal bunkmate, from Tee's perspective. Jay had a different perspective. He was not happy having Tee as his bunkmate.

On their first day of training, Jay had pulled Tee off to the side in the barracks and said in a harsh whisper, "I don't want you as a bunkmate. Quit now and stop wasting everyone's time."

Tee locked eyes with him. Looking upward at a steep angle, he calmly said, "I will get through this whether you want me as a bunkmate or not. We're bunkmates until you quit," parroting what Dee had said. Tee then turned around and walked off.

Jay was taken aback. He wasn't sure what he expected Tee to do, but turning the tables on him, staring him down, wasn't it. Tee didn't seem to be intimidated by him at all. That put him in rare company and earned some private grudging respect.

It was a truce of sorts. Other bunkmates shared stories, joked, practiced together in the rare downtimes, and most seemed to be on the path to becoming good friends. Jay was a good bunkmate when it was required. But nothing more. It was obvious to the other recruits that Jay was not happy with Tee. It was also obvious after a few days of competitive training that Jay was likely the top recruit among them. This led to Tee getting increasingly harassed. Recruits with weak bunkmates had gotten the idea that when their bunkmate quit, they might get Jay if Tee quit at the same time.

Tee was taking a shower when he heard a voice say, "Time to quit you little shit."

Tee hunched over a little and breathed out with a sigh. *Why do I keep getting compared to excrement?* he wondered. At least it rhymes, which shows some creativity. The speaker was Kale. His bunkmate had quit the day before. He was the clear runner up to Jay in the recruiting class. Jay and Kale would make an unbeatable team. Tee just continued his shower and didn't respond.

"I said it's time to quit," Kale said as he stepped closer.

Tee turned to him, looked him squarely in the eyes and calmly said, "I'm not going to quit."

"You're going to regret not taking my advice," Kale said with menace as he moved within reach of Tee.

"You touch him, and you'll have me to deal with," Jay said as he entered the shower room. Everyone paused, showering to watch this play out.

"Why do you care Jay? He's just holding you back," Kale replied, trying to reason with Jay.

"He's my bunkmate. If you attack him, you attack me," Jay said firmly.

"Okay, Jay. But you're going to regret not doing what you can to get rid of him," Kale said with disgust and then walked away.

Tee was privately relieved. The harassment had been escalating and there were too many times when Jay wasn't around. Making a statement like that in a shower room full of recruits meant the story would go everywhere. Nobody took Jay lightly. They wouldn't risk his wrath.

"Thanks, Jay," said Tee in a low voice.

"Don't thank me. I'm just doing my job. Make sure you do yours," Jay said sternly and walked away.

The next day, the first two weeks' point awards were posted. Jay was on top, and Tee was not far behind him.

Jay had consistently won various competitions during the week. Tee had come in first every day on the morning run. He also outscored everybody by a huge margin in archery. This impressed some while disgusting others who believed that archery was for women and old men.

The Guard tied bunkmates together in everything. If your bunkmate won points, you were automatically awarded half of what they had earned. The same was true for point deductions. If your bed wasn't made correctly, or your uniform wasn't perfect, or you came up short on a thousand other trivial details, you both lost points. Sometimes points were deducted because Dee didn't like the way you looked.

"How in God's name did Tee Stone accumulate so many points?" Dee bellowed. He was incensed. That skinny little kid hadn't quit yet and was near the top in point totals.

Sergeant Derick shook his head and said, "If you remember, we put a high bonus on endurance and speed for the morning run because of the poor endurance this recruit class came in with. Tee has won the morning run by a wide margin every day. When we did the mountain run, it was even worse. If it were just the runs, he would be in the middle of the pack. But Jay is winning the majority of the sparring sessions, so Tee gets points from that too."

"Okay, it's just the first two weeks after all," Dee said, "Let's take the bonus away and downgrade points for the morning run. I don't want the endurance runs to award so many points going forward. Keep them practicing their archery. Griff was right to insist Guard members be competent with all weapons of war. But we don't have to give significant points for it. We aren't Wall Archers after all. Two more weeks and we'll be ramping down the heavy exercise. After that weapons training will start along with team competitions. Jay will not appreciate going from winning to losing."

"The kid is scrawny, but he's tough, Dee. He was blue and confused when he got out of the stream march exercise. I was worried we'd lose him. I'm not sure he'll quit. I also heard Jay let it be known that an attack on Tee was an attack on himself. Nobody is going to poke that bear," Sergeant Derick said.

Dee sighed and said, "I heard that too. Have to admit it makes me even more impressed with Jay. Tee is a major problem for him, but he's being a good bunkmate. Best traditions of the Guard and all that. On the bright side, with team competitions, it's going to get even more challenging having the wrong bunkmate."

CHAPTER 14

FRESHMEN ORIENTATION

Matthews, Chair of the mathematics department strolled into Del's office, plopped down in a chair, and said, "I'm not sure there is anything we can teach Quinn."

"What do you mean?" Del asked, confused.

"The first day after class, he came to my office and said with that big cheesy grin of his that he had a few corrections to submit for our textbooks. I thought great. When Quinn doesn't understand something, he is going to waste my time claiming the book is wrong. I have to admit, I cursed your name when that thought crossed my mind," Matthews said.

Del's eyebrows came together, and he asked, "So what happened next?"

"I was busy, so I told him to come back the next week and we would discuss it. After looking over his proposed corrections, I pulled Newton in. We spent the next few days checking and rechecking his work. While a few were simple typos, most were legitimate errors no one had spotted before. One was an obscure mistake in an incredibly dense derivation in differential geometry that hurts my head just thinking about it."

"Was he right?"

"Yes. We substantiated all of his claimed errors.

Newton and I decided Quinn ought to be teaching our higher math courses instead of the two of us. The only problem with pulling him into the math department is his claim that 'math is easy and boring.' He only likes it because it's a tool he can use to do 'interesting things.' He told Newton and I this with such joy and delight that it was even more insulting than it sounds. And I thought bland and monotone Dorothy was irritating."

"So how did he get the knowledge? They don't teach that in high school."

"I asked him that. Turns out Dorothy has been checking out textbooks from the university library on her regular trips down here. She's been home schooling Quinn and Hestie since they were in grade school. My guess is that home schooling Quinn consists of handing him books."

"So, what do you and Newton propose we do?" Del asked.

"Newton and I will sign off on Quinn satisfying requirements for an advanced degree in math when he completes his non-math requirements. We did our due diligence in a day long exam. By the end of the day, all the blackboards in the room were filled and Newton and I were feeling stupid. Quinn passed, but I think we failed," Matthews said with a wry smile. "He actually turned the test around and started asking us questions we couldn't answer. Then he gleefully supplied the answers. I think he thought we were all just having fun."

"Okay, I wondered how much of the lower-level course work he would test out of. Let's do this. His passion is engineering. I will pull the department together and come up with a plan. I suspect he will test out of most classes like he did in math. If so, I have a number of challenging special projects he can be assigned to. He will still need to take his required courses in the other subjects. Rounding him out can only be good. I think I'll pull in Phillis from the social work department and see if there is anything we can do to improve his social awareness. He is a happy and bubbly version of his mother, and you already mentioned how irritating that is at times."

"Yeah, nobody likes their stupidity pointed out to them. Especially when it's pointed out with such enthusiasm," Matthews said with a smile. "By the way, Newton and I decided over drinks that we will always have our PhDs to separate us from Quinn. He would never waste his time doing anything as easy and boring as that," Matthews said.

Del smiled and said, "If nothing else, Dorothy and her son will help keep all our egos in check."

"Amen to that," Matthews said with a smile.

Phillis, the dean of the social work department, was in Del's graduation class years ago. She was a dark, complected woman who exuded calmness wherever she went. Phillis had a way of listening that encouraged you to tell her your innermost thoughts. She seemed to understand everything you said. She seemed to be interested. Del had walked away from conversations with her in the past, wondering how in the world she had gotten some private part of him exposed. So, he was always a bit cautious approaching her.

"Good morning, Del. It's good to see you," she said in a way that indicated to him that she really was glad to see him.

"Good morning Phillis, hope all is well with you," Del responded cautiously. "I came by to talk to you about

Quinn Espers, Dorothy's son."

"Oh. What did you want to discuss?" she said with a concerned smile.

"I wanted to get your advice on what we can do to help with his social integration here at the university," Del said a bit cryptically.

Phillis laughed softly with eyes bright. Her laugh had a bell-like tone. It really was quite endearing. "That's an interesting way to put it, Del." Then her features warmed and with compassion she said, "I've met both Quinn and Hestie. Of course, I know Dorothy quite well. Probably the best thing we can do is set up some interaction coaching for Quinn."

"What's that?" Del asked.

"It starts with a psychological evaluation to understand how Quinn sees the world and reacts to it. We then work with him to understand how others see him and techniques he can use to avoid making them uncomfortable. Most likely, he doesn't understand why his blunt, truthful statements bother others. If so, he will likely appreciate blunt statements in return and act on them. I get along with Dorothy really well. She is a very compassionate and caring person. It's just hard for most people to see it," Phillis said.

"Dorothy, compassionate?" Del said with surprise.

"Yes. She loves her husband and kids fiercely. The work she does assisting university researchers is because she cares about the students and wants to help them. Most of their research doesn't really interest her all that much. Ask around Apple Valley and they'll tell you she's a saint. Your kid's sick at 3:00 AM? Just go knock on the Espers's door and Dorothy will walk back with you for a house call. She just referred a woman and child to me for trauma counseling to help them deal with years of physical and emotional abuse. She found an older woman willing to take them into her home until they get settled. Most doctors would just suggest their patient seek counseling. They wouldn't worry about things like accommodations. Dorothy made sure they were taken care of and safe," Phillis observed.

"I would never have guessed that," Del said with surprise.

"Well, perhaps you should pay closer attention to social cues," Phillis said with a gleam in her eye.

"So, you're comparing my lack of seeing the real Dorothy with Dorothy's lack of social awareness," Del said with a small frown.

"Yes, that's exactly it. It's good to see you making progress," Phillis said with an even bigger smile. Del appreciated her wit, but quickly clamped down on that appreciation. Then Phillis gracefully said, "With Dorothy, you have to get past the flat affect and language she uses. Look at her actions and work your way back to what her motivations must be. This is true for everyone. But it's especially critical in understanding people with Dorothy's personality. To help Dorothy understand you, avoid tact and tell her the unvarnished truth. She won't be insulted; she will be appreciative. I know it seems counter intuitive, but most people want to be communicated with in the manner they themselves communicate."

"Should I do the same with Quinn?" Del asked.

"Let me spend some time with him and get back to you," Phillis said. "I'm guessing yes. But he has a sister who is super empathetic and some of that awareness may have rubbed off on him. It might change the plan a little bit. By the way, I've been trying to talk Hestie into social work. She has enormous potential. Unfortunately for me, she wants to focus more on the medical end of things. That got me thinking again about the connection between the two.

"Many times, when someone calls on a doctor, it's an emotional or life choice issue that needs attention. Doctors need to recognize this and respond accordingly. I would like to propose upgrading our medical degrees with social work classes designed to help them recognize when a problem may have its origins in something not strictly medical."

"Okay, Phillis, that does make sense. I'm not sure the medical board is open to more requirements right now. But putting it in front of them can't hurt. Let me know when you have a proposal on how to help Quinn."

"I will, Del, take care of yourself," she said with warmth.

He knew it wasn't just words. She meant it. Which warmed him. That woman was dangerous. He needed to avoid her as much as possible.

CHAPTER 15

AFTER HELL

The day started early with the good news that IH was officially over. They were told to quickly pack up because they were moving from their high valley training grounds to their main training camp. This was located below the Landfall Dam and just behind the Wall. The peninsula consisted of three regions spilling downhill, starting at the highest elevation in Apple Valley.

The two lower valleys had dams defining their southernmost boundary, with large lakes and broad fields. The valleys all had spectacular steep mountains on each side, with a few smaller valleys in the mountains on each side spilling into them. The two lower valleys were agricultural, with towns and a few cities dotting the landscape.

After a few hours of double time march, Tee worried that After Hell might be worse than In Hell. Tee's thoughts drifted to Grammy, and then to her advice to "Enjoy it." He looked up from the trail and realized how beautiful it was. The narrow trail followed a swiftly moving stream swelled with glacial melt and surrounded by green forest-covered hills. Eventually, the trail rounded a corner, and a stunning view of Landfall Valley far below appeared. This was an adventure. He had the choice to embrace and enjoy it, even if it was physically challenging.

Under his breath he said, "Thanks, Grammy."

The trail continued snaking its way alongside the steepening slopes of the stream, then widened out with another view of the Landfall Valley below. Just barely visible was a city sitting on the northeast end of a large lake. This was Tee's first glimpse of Landfall City. Hestie and Quinn were living there now and attending university. Of course, he wouldn't get to visit the city until Shake Out was over. He was really looking forward to seeing his two friends as soon as he could.

A sudden pang of homesickness hit him as he wondered how everyone was doing. This eventually had his mind wandering back to Diana with the familiar anxiety that caused. He slapped himself mentally and again elicited Grammy's advice. Life was wonderful, and this was a grand adventure.

They reduced down to march cadence once they entered the valley. The road was well maintained, flat, and easy to march on. Tee decided they had double marched them through the mountains because it was difficult. He had to admit they were better at it when it ended than when it began.

Late in the afternoon, they passed through Landfall City, skirting the lake until they reached the dam. From there, it was a switchback road down alongside the dam, ending in a canyon at the bottom. At the top of the road, Tee got his first glimpse of the Wall. It dominated the end of the canyon and was impressive. The canyon in between was entirely dedicated to military purposes and was a buffer between the GEMs and the dam. It included a small city to supply labor and support for the warehouses stuffed with weapons, food, and materials of all kinds needed for the defense of the Wall. Separate from the city, and near the Wall, was the main camp and headquarters for the Guard.

The area between the base of the dam and the Wall was sandy, hot, and very dry. The Landfall Dam had spillways that could direct water over cliffs directly into the ocean or down the natural waterway that had existed before the dam was built. Dumping the overflow into the ocean prevented the GEMs from having a local source of fresh water to support their attacks.

They finally reached their new camp in the late afternoon. The good news was that they had a much better bunk bed. Jay had walked in and claimed one off in a corner, away from the bathroom. Their old one had almost been in the bathroom. They had spent all of IH dealing with the dampness, smells, and noise. While the barracks didn't have privacy anywhere, their old spot was basically on the highway of recruits going back and forth to the bathroom at all hours of the day and night.

The room in the new barracks was identical to the one in the mountains, so the owners of that particular spot objected. Jay told them this was a new camp and so all the bunks were open until claimed. This ended up sparking an argument and mad scramble for bunk beds, getting louder and louder until Dee walked briskly into the barracks and said, "What in God's name is going on?"

"Salad stole our bunk bed," came the answer. Many of the bunkmate teams had nicknames given out by the instructors. It was a compliment of sorts because it meant you had been recognized. Not having a name meant you were beneath contempt. Salad was a derogatory name for Jay and Tee. One of the standard items for lunch was an apple and grape salad. The joke went that Jay was the apple because he was always sunburned, and Tee was the grape because he was always sporting purple bruises. It also referenced the comical size difference between them.

"If it's yours, take it back," said Dee, looking as if he expected them to do that right there and then. Silence was his only answer.

Dee stared at the complaining bunkmates for a while then said with a sneering smile, "Well, looks like it's not yours then." The two turned around and joined the scramble for a new bunk bed.

The demanding physical activities did ramp down, but stayed at a high level. More and more time was spent developing hand-to-hand skills and introducing weapons training. There were additional instructors now that the goal was to improve the recruits' skills in a wide range of capabilities. Midnight marches were few and far between, but common enough that you couldn't depend on getting a full night's sleep.

Tee was in the best shape of his life. He was also putting on quite a bit of muscle, which surprised him, given his slender frame. This motivated him to work even harder in his spare time, as strength was his biggest deficiency. His hand-to-hand combat instructors told him they were going to concentrate on defensive skills. In other words, you have no business attacking anyone. Tee thought this was a mistake, but he took what instruction he could get and practiced hard.

While individual combat was always a focus, teamwork was increasingly emphasized. Two on two sparring with short sword and shield had been going on for over two weeks with Tee and Jay having some success. Without discussing it with Jay, Tee had decided the best course of action was for him to delay his opponent long enough for Jay to win his bout and then double up on the remaining adversary. He could engage enough to protect Jay's back without risking a quick loss for himself. This culminated in an end of phase competition with a high number of points to be awarded to the winning team. Second place would get nothing. Dee had barked out the point rules for this event, "Fighting is about winning; we don't award points to losers."

They had gotten to the finals with a combination of luck, extraordinary skill, and effort. Primarily on Jay's part. Tee had done a good job of staying alive long enough for Jay to free up and double team Tee's opponent. They narrowly won the last few rounds.

Now, however, they were going to go up against Kale and his bunkmate Zeb. This pair had been racing up the point totals while Tee and Jay had been slowly going in the opposite direction. While Jay had the edge on Kale, he wouldn't be able to put him down easily or quickly. Zeb, on the other hand, was nearly at Kales level and would easily dispatch Tee.

While Kale and Zeb had quickly dispatched their respective opponents. Jay and Tee's bouts had been messy affairs, with Jay basically having to win two fights. Jay was exhausted. Kale and Zeb were openly bragging that they were going to steal Jay and Tee's strategy by defeating Tee fast and then doubling up on Jay. There was no doubt in anyone's mind how this was going to turn out.

"Do you want to concede? You have zero chance, Jay; it will just be embarrassing. Everybody is watching, you know." Kale smiled, taunting him as they lined up to start.

Dee had shrunk the circle for the final round, declaring, "I want to see a good fight. That means I don't want to watch Tee run around all over the place." Dee had clearly understood the strategy Tee employed and decided to eliminate it. Tee, having gotten used to Dee's insults, just ignored the comment.

Zeb smiled meanly at Tee and said, "You're dead in ten seconds," which Tee realized was probably true if he didn't think of something quick.

The whistle blew and Tee dropped his sword and, holding his shield in front of him with both hands, darted sideways past Zeb. He charged right into the side of a surprised Kale, knocking him to the ground. Kale had reacted quickly, scoring a kill on Tee as they went down. But, in doing so, it opened him up to Jay, who darted in and scored a killing blow of his own. That left Jay and Zeb to fight it out one on one. It was a good fight, but Jay eventually won.

The crowd of recruits erupted. Some were delighted with the trickery, but some were offended. A voice in the crowd shouted, "That wasn't fair!"

Dee bellowed out, silencing them. "There is no fair in a fight. The only rules we have in recruit training are for the quitters. We have safety rules in place, so they have a chance to be useful citizens after they leave. Sacrificing yourself for the good of the team is in the best traditions of the Guard. And in case you're confused, whining is not."

That Dee had actually given him a compliment had momentarily swelled Tee's chest with pride. Dee then ruined it by observing, "That cheap trick will only work once, Jay." With that parting comment, Dee turned and walked off.

Jay walked over to Tee, let out a big sigh, and said, "That was smart. You surprised me as much as you surprised them. I almost didn't react fast enough."

Tee hesitated, checking Jay's face twice, looking for

sarcasm, smiled, then said with a grin, "So, I'm not completely wasting your time."

Jay was startled by Tee's response. He had changed his mind about Tee. With the world against him, the little guy had steadfastly moved forward, regardless of the odds. He had to admit that Tee was hard not to like. And by now, pretty much everyone respected him. Perhaps he was due a little ribbing.

"No, not completely," he said with a smile, then turned serious and said, "Let's start planning these bouts, agreed?"

"Sounds good to me. The other bunkmates have weaknesses we can take advantage of. We aren't the only team with a major deficiency," Tee said, getting Jay to smile again with the obvious self-deprecating reference to himself.

As they walked back to the barracks both basking in the win, Tee suddenly turned serious and asked, "Could we trade knowledge as well?"

"What do you mean?" asked Jay, confused.

"You teach me how to fight and I'll point out weaknesses," Tee said with a grin.

"Weaknesses?" asked Jay.

"How do you think I win the occasional match? It isn't because I'm a better fighter. I study everyone to figure out their strengths, weaknesses, and tendencies. It's the only advantage I have."

He had to admit it was surprising Tee won any matches. Thinking back, he realized that although Tee lost most of his sparring sessions; he had enough wins for it to be something other than luck. Jay was also reflective enough to realize he was winging it most of the time. While he was good at reacting to situations, having a plan with contingencies to go along with that would probably be an improvement. "Okay, I'm in," said Jay.

The Salad team was going to give him a heart attack. Dee had announced a bonus for the team winning the first bunkmates' competition with weapons. He had done that to put more distance between the Fish and Salad teams. Kale and Zeb were called the Fish because Zeb had failed his initial swimming test. While not required for entrance, it was a required skill to graduate from IH. The instructors had roused both Zeb and his original bunkmate extra early to practice swimming in the freezing cold lake every morning for a week until Zeb passed. Thus, Dee started calling them the Fish. Kale had inherited the name when he joined Zeb.

Salad winning the first bunkmates' competition had backfired, putting them back in the lead. Before this fiasco, Tee had been below the cutoff with little chance of catching up. Now he was in the mix again and it would take continued manipulation on Dee's part to fix it.

Over the next few weeks, Dee carefully picked opponents and situations so Jay would earn enough points to stay solidly in the top fifty while limiting what Tee earned. It had gotten to the point where even the other teams noticed.

When Jay first realized this, he was dead set on confronting Dee. "That SOB is doing everything he can to knock you down. I'm going to go tell him what I think about that," Jay said with fury in his voice.

"It won't change anything, Jay. He's in charge and doing what he thinks best. Getting a rise out of either one of us will just encourage him. Let's prove him wrong instead."

Training had progressed from small to large squad training in realistic scenarios. The goal was to quickly form up, select a sergeant in charge, access the situation, and deploy. Central to their training was how to attack or defend a wall. Pacifica's strategy was based on defending cliff side fortifications and the Wall. The Wall was Pacifica's weakness, so a major focus of training.

Getting near the end of the Shake Out, Dee was carefully selecting Tee and Jay's opponents to get the result he wanted. He and his instructor core had completely failed to get Tee to quit. Worse, Jay and Tee had formed a close friendship which provided Tee with a supporter who could make a difference. Dee remembered his own Shake Out and understood. It was you and your bunkmate against the world. That tended to form close and lasting relationships. Jay would make the point total with just individual contests, so didn't need the bunkmate points. Tee, on the other hand, needed them. In fact, he was below the top fifty cut list again with little hope of making it.

At the end of another long day of weapons training, Tee was sitting in a tub full of hot water. He thought he could feel every muscle in his body. As the hot water did its job, a pleasurable dull ache took over. Strange how wonderful it was to go from the physical pain of IH to the feeling of bliss that came from working out to his limit, but not beyond. Sergeant Derick alternated them between ice baths and hot baths, driven by a carefully designed workout schedule. Since the Salad team did everything together, they were on the same schedule, although concentrating on improving different physical attributes.

"This is heaven," Jay said with a big sigh. "I love this as much as I hate ice baths."

"Grammy tells me to find enjoyment in everything," teased Tee.

"Your grammy sounds as crazy as you," Jay said, hesitated, and then added, "You realize you're crazy, right?"

Tee looked over with a wry smile and said, "It's been suggested a few times, yeah." Tee let out a big sigh and asked, "What does your dad do in the Guard, Jay?"

"He was a large squad staff sergeant, fourteen members. They focused on destroying siege towers, battering rams, and anything else that gets built on our side of the moat. He's now in phase one of retirement acting as a recruit combat instructor," Jay said.

"Why isn't he here?" Tee asked.

"When an instructor has a kid in recruit training, they take a break and wait until the next class. The Guard doesn't want any hint of preference."

"I guess that explains your skills," Tee said. "Who gave you the invite to join?"

"Griff. I've known him since I was a little kid. I wouldn't say he's a friend of my dad's. According to him, Griff doesn't have any friends. Well, none that are alive. The story is that when his mentor disappeared, Griff sort of went mental. Already intense, he became obsessed with improving all facets of the Guard. His mentor was master sergeant when he disappeared, and Griff was the obvious choice to replace him."

"Do you have any idea why he gave me an invite," Tee said hopefully. He really couldn't figure it out.

"He must hate you for some reason," Jay said, smiling, then he turned serious and said, "I was angry and confused when you showed up. I just knew Griff must have been the one to invite you. He has a reputation for shaking things up, which isn't appreciated by everyone in the Guard. It took a while, but I think I understand why. Your instincts and ability to plan an attack or defense based on an enemy's strengths and weaknesses are what he wants. It's unique. I heard him tell Dad one time that the Guard should be more than a bunch of brutes bashing about. Coming from the head brute that seemed strange and funny. I can remember my dad and I laughing about it. I think I get it now."

"So, you're saying Griff isn't a complete idiot and neither am I," Tee said with a smile.

"You need to stop making fun of yourself. It gets irritating. Accept an honest compliment when it's offered," Jay said with a frown.

Tee hesitated, took a deep breath, sighed, and said, "You're right. It does feel good to be appreciated. It's just hard for me to take a compliment. Thank you, Jay."

After a few minutes of silence, Jay asked, "So, what are we going to do with the large squad exercise tomorrow?" Once they had started planning their bouts, Jay quickly realized Tee was an incredible strategist. His plans didn't always work, but they were always well thought out. They had a chance of success even in no-win situations. Tee and Jay eventually converged on a division of responsibility to take advantage of each other's strengths. Tee would put together a general plan with contingencies and Jay would execute it. That meant Jay would assume the role of sergeant when a squad was formed, making all the real-time decisions once engaged.

"My guess is that Dee will have us go first and give us teams with generally weak offensive skills. Then he will assign us to take the Wall. We'll likely go up against Fish and teams with strong offensive skills," Tee speculated.

"Why offensive if they are assigned to protect the Wall?" Jay asked.

"Dee doesn't just want us to fail to capture the Wall. He wants us to get decimated below the Wall. Embarrassment is what he's after," Tee said.

"Sounds like he might get what he wants."

"It's okay, Kale will take charge of their squad."

"I don't understand why that's good news," Jay said in confusion. Tee gave him a knowing smile until Jay's face slowly transformed into a smile and said, "I know that look. What's your plan?"

It was another bright, cool day that promised to heat up quickly. At first muster, they saw they had an audience today. Everyone recognized Griff, and most recognized the CGG. All the instructors were there in person as well. With one week to go, this looked like a final exam of sorts.

For the past few weeks, their training had taken place at the training Wall. This was an 800-foot-long replica of the real Wall. The only difference was that it had more posterns, or small doors, than the actual wall. The small doors provide an element of surprise, as a squad can pop out quickly and have multiple locations for a retreat. Since the recruits knew where all the posterns were, more of them simulated the ability to stage a surprise attack from the Wall.

Dee explained how the large squad exercise would work. "For the next two days, you will be formed into squads of ten bunkmates each. Each day, two squads will be named and assigned to either attack or defend the training Wall. You will have ten minutes to form up, choose your leadership, and come up with a plan. The exercise will end in two hours unless it ends sooner because the attackers have captured the Wall, or the defenders have decimated the attacking squad. We will then muster for a critique from your instructors. Any questions?"

They had all learned that awful first day that asking Dee questions meant you either "hadn't been listening" or "you wanted to waste everyone's time." So, after a few seconds of dead silence, Dee gave the instructions. "Today the Defend squad will be Fish, Stumble, Tree, Baffled, Reckless, Flee, Dense, Annoy, Feeble, and Oh No. The attack squad will be Salad, Neander, Witless, Late, Nervous, Sloth, Reek, Scum, and Squirrel. You have your instructions. You are excused." He then turned and looked right at Jay and Tee with glee leaking onto his face.

As they turned to go, Jay carefully guarded his features and said in a whisper, "You are one scary dude, Tee." They both smiled.

Jay quickly pulled the nine other bunkmate teams together and declared, "I'm in charge. Any questions?" There was a grunt or two, but no real opposition. Jay had that effect on people. They would have voted him leader anyway, so the direct approach simply saved them time. "Now listen up. Tee will explain the plan."

Tee turned to face everyone and said, "The plan depends on Kale being chosen to lead the squad. As you know, he is a solid leader and a tremendous fighter. He's also super aggressive and will look for a quick kill. We are going to take advantage of his lack of patience. We will grab scaling ladders and attack to the left of the Portcullis. But it needs to be a lackluster attack, with Jay and a reserve holding back. Act confused, argue with each other, look frustrated and defeated. Get a few scaling ladders up but let them throw them back down.

"At some point, Kale will get tired of waiting and order an all-out attack through the Portcullis. When they do, Jay is going to call a retreat. Let them collapse your right flank and retreat toward the left flank in a sweeping movement. Stay close in a good defense. The left flank will attempt—but fail—to envelop the attack by controlling the base of the Wall in an obvious attempt to take the portcullis. Moose, Rilla, and I will duck down behind the line of boulders and get split off from the right flank as it collapses.

"Once their attention is distracted by the sudden envelopment attack, we will sneak away from the skirmish and down the Wall, away from the action."

Moose and Rilla were collectively called Neander, which was short for Neanderthal. This was an old earth pre-human known for its robustness. Dee assigned the name to insinuate they weren't quite human. It was not a compliment. He even gave Moose and Rilla their nicknames. They were the only two in their recruit class he had done this to. Rilla was short for Gorilla. What did ring true is that they were both extremely strong and had an oddly prehistoric sort of look to them.

"We will retreat to the sixth postern. It will look like we're trying a rear assault with too few warriors. Once we are in position, Jay will call for a mass charge, followed quickly by a retreat back to a packed line. This time, while they are distracted, Neander will hook hands and throw me to the top of the Wall. I'll open the postern, and we'll attack the back of the Portcullis and lock the attacking defenders out below the Wall. If we accomplish this, the exercise will have ended, and we win."

"Sounds like a suicide mission," said Moose.

"Tee specializes in suicide missions," Jay said, smiling at Tee, then turning serious, "It's that or a protracted fight below the Wall that we lose. We all know we're outmatched."

"We're betting they commit to an all-out attack and leave minimal Guards for the Portcullis. Best-case scenario is they ignore us while we circle behind them and don't see me get thrown up onto the Wall," Tee explained.

Dee was standing on the observation platform with Griff and the CGG when the whistle blew. They all watched the slowly developing unorganized attack with Dee huffing and puffing, clearly disgusted. "You would think after all the training they've had, they could mount a decent attack. This is embarrassing," Dee said angrily.

"I'm sure that's what the Defend team is thinking," said Griff blandly.

Just then, the Portcullis burst open and the Defend team surged out, driving the Attack team backward. They watched as the Attack team's left flank tried to envelop the attack and force it toward their right flank in an obvious attempt to threaten the Portcullis. It was unsuccessful. The result was a tight defensive line angled with the attackers' backs toward the Portcullis and the Wall beyond it.

"Well, look at that. Tee left his bunkmate and is running away with Neander. Some sort of rear attack?" Dee said with a sneer. "Just more incompetence."

"The left flank envelopment failure has set the line so that none of the Defend team are paying attention to their rear," said Griff. Again in a bland voice.

They continued to watch the slow systematic destruction of the Attack team. Then Griff observed with a chuckle. "Don't look now, but Neander just threw Tee up on the Wall. Looks like they overdid it a bit."

Tee hit the inside railing wall hard. He slowly crawled to his feet, slowly shaking his head. His vision cleared, the pain subsided, and he suddenly remembered what he needed to do. Careful to keep hidden from the Guards, he made his way down inside the Wall. He opened up the sixth Postern and now there were three of the Attack team inside the Wall.

Dee watched dumbfounded as the three of them surprised the two guards watching the final stages of the assault from just inside an open Portcullis. After dispatching the guards, they shut and locked the Portcullis, climbed to the top of the Wall, and declared victory. The recruits watching all this went wild.

Dee had the recruits form up below the observation deck for a critique. In his usual brusque fashion, he looked directly at Kale and asked in a sneering voice, "What did you learn?"

Kale looked up at Dee with a forlorn look, hesitated a moment, and then, in a clear voice, said, "It's better to be on Tee's team." The crowd standing around broke into loud and prolonged, uproarious laughter. Dee scowled but then failed to keep a tight smile off his face.

At week's end, they marched up to Armstrong Reservoir, just above the capital. It was an artificial lake created by the original colonizers to provide clean water for the city. It was in a relatively small but wide valley that was also maintained as a nature park with numerous trails spiderwebbing across forest land on both sides of the lake. They had spent a week at the reserve earlier in their training as part of their scouting basics. Everyone was familiar with the layout.

At one end of the lake was a long dam and at the

other, a single trail connected the two sides. When they arrived, they set up camp and goofed around like the young men they were. Training was almost over. Tomorrow, they would participate in their last exercise. After that, they would either go home or be Guard members for life.

As soon as Tee saw the forest, he wanted to go on a hike. Nothing relaxed him as much as the quiet solitude of the forest. Jay decided he would go with him, even though he didn't understand why anyone would want to simply walk around in the woods. He was a city boy.

"Well, it's almost over," Jay said.

"Yeah, can't believe we'll be done after tomorrow," Tee replied.

"Are you sure you can pull off your end?" Jay asked.

"Not a problem. Just get to the choke point as soon as possible. Anyone you can defeat on our list will help the point total."

"However this goes tomorrow, Tee, you're stopping by to meet my family on Sunday before you head home," Jay said.

"Don't worry. We're both going to make the cut and continue training. Just make sure you do your part."

"I'm never going to hear the end of that, am I?" Jay said with a grin.

"No, you're not." And they both smiled.

Dee was up early, as usual. He found pleasure in being up before everyone else, enjoying the quiet of the morning. He thought this was the best recruitment class he had ever produced. It was something to be proud of. It was also the strangest. Dee wasn't the reflective type.

He spent his time in the here and now, working to achieve his objectives. Every problem had an answer. Mistakes were merely a mechanism for learning.

When he heard people talk about the gray areas, he interpreted that as an excuse for not being able to make decisions. He knew most in the Guard thought him to be insensitive and uncaring. Nothing could be further from the truth. He cared deeply for his recruits. Whenever he heard one had gone down at the Wall, he wondered what he could do better with the next batch of recruits.

His real problem with Tee was that he would never be able to forgive himself if one of his boys died, because Tee didn't measure up. Once they graduated, they all became his boys. He never called them that out loud, but that was how he felt about them.

Contrary to all evidence, Dee had developed a high level of respect for Tee. Although he respected everyone who made it through recruit training, he had special regard for him. He was tough! Dee wasn't sure he could have overcome the challenges that had been thrown at Tee.

Well, after today it will be over.

Jay will make it no matter what happens, and Tee would have to race around the lake in record time, encountering no one. He had set up the staged release in opposite order of their endurance run point totals. Tee would leave last, which meant he had a gauntlet to get through, as everyone would challenge him to spar if they saw him. He might finish, but it would be really slow and not enough to get over the hump.

This last competition was constructed to test the recruits' scouting abilities. The day started on the south side of the lake at the dam. It would end sometime two to three days later at the north end of the dam. A large bonus of points was reserved for the first ten recruits to make it around the lake to the end point. These points were ratioed by the difference in arrival times, so relative speed was highly rewarded. Some of the trails had instructors positioned as pickets. If you failed to spot them, your day was over. If another recruit spotted you, they could challenge, and the loser's day would be over. You only got points if you or your bunkmate finished.

The recruits were assembled and ready to go. It was a cool, windless morning as the valley became visible in the dawn. No clouds in the sky and not a ripple on the lake. A perfect day, Dee thought. Dee and Griff were watching Sergeant Derick release the recruits one at a time. As they were called up, Dee would give a short description of the recruits' strengths and weaknesses with his recommendation for the next phase of training. When Jay's turn came, Dee turned to Griff and said, "That may be our next master sergeant."

Griff turned, nodded, and said, "He certainly has all the physical attributes. I liked what I saw during the Wall exercise. He carried out the ruse perfectly. We'll put him on a non-com training program, then wait and see what happens in real action."

Dee winched at the ruse reference and then eventually said, "I understand why you invited Tee. His ability to outmaneuver his opponents is impressive, unique even. He's gained the respect of everyone. However, he's not going to make it."

"Explain to me why you're so opposed to having him in the Guard," Griff said without malice.

"If he's in the Guard, and below the Wall, somebody

is going to die because he can't do his part," Dee responded.

Griff nodded thoughtfully and said, "I understand your concern, but I disagree with your conclusion." He hesitated, then added, "I do admire your passion and hard work to ensure every Guard recruit is able to step up to the challenges."

It was a rare acknowledgement from Griff, and Dee appreciated it. Griff could be very hard on people, which Dee also appreciated. It took a little of the sting out of a feeling that he had been unfair to Tee, and Jay for that matter. But in his mind, the integrity of the Guard needed to be protected at all costs.

When at last Tee's name was called Dee went through his analysis. "Tough, smart, but with significant physical limitations. He shows an aptitude for scouting in the wild. Best in his class. Scout Instructor Walker was very impressed. Perhaps his hunting experience. His inability to win individual sparring matches will disqualify him from the Guard after today based on points. His real value is as a strategist. I will strongly recommend him for volunteer corp. officer training. Your recommendations for making a few of these roles full-time jobs make sense to me. Perhaps he is the natural place to start."

Dee noticed that Griff was looking over his shoulder at something behind him and smiling. That wasn't good. Dee turned around and watched Tee finish taking off his clothes. He folded them, then placed them with his boots into the waterproof backpack the recruits had been issued. He had taken out his food and water to make room and discarded them. He put the backpack on and tied the front straps together tightly. Then Tee, completely naked with a backpack snuggly strapped to his back, turned toward them and smiled.

"Is he giving up? Is this some kind of protest?" Dee asked, confused.

"Maybe he's too warm. Perhaps he's not hungry," Griff said, his sarcasm heightening Dee's concern.

Then they both watched him turn around and casually walk down to the lake, wade in, and start swimming swiftly for the other side.

Dee was speechless. He had never seen anyone swim like that. He remembered back to when the recruits passed their tests. He clearly remembered Tee splashing around wildly with everyone else and finishing in the middle of the pack. Now he was swimming swiftly and smoothly with what looked like little effort.

Griff interrupted Dee's astonishment by saying, "Looks like Tee might set a new record."

"That's not possible. And if it is, it's got to be against the rules. This is clearly a race around the lake, not across it," Dee spluttered.

"Crossing the dam is forbidden, but there isn't a rule prohibiting swimming across. We had a recruit try to paddle a log across, remember? We had to go find a boat and save him. The idiot almost drowned. But we only added a rule that the recruits couldn't use logs or rafts to cross the lake. There is no restriction on swimming across." Griff's smile widened.

"You knew he could do this," Dee said, glaring at Griff.

"I always do a thorough investigation before I invite anyone to recruit training," Griff admitted.

"This is wrong," Dee said, glaring.

"You're right, it is wrong. It's also wrong for you to manipulate point awards to unfairly drive someone out.

So, we're even," Griff said calmly.

Dee knew he had been outmaneuvered. Tee would get an outrageous number of points for this. It explained why Griff hadn't been complaining about Dee playing games with the point system. One or more of the instructors must have told Griff long ago. Dee took a deep breath and relaxed. He often told the recruits that it's better to be smarter than stronger than your opponent. It wasn't lost on him that he didn't say that as often to this class. Tee was going to become one of his boys, and as such, he would worry about him like all the others. Perhaps even more so.

CHAPTER 16

INDUCTION CEREMONY

Your father would be so proud of you, thought Arti. He took jibes for being short but never let it affect him. You have his charisma, which seems to serve you well. In many ways, you really did get the best of us. Arti knew the Guard functions were lavish affairs. This, however, was even grander than she imagined. Being a member of the Guard was difficult for families. The constant worry about safety combined with frequent absences was a burden few appreciated. The annual induction ceremony was just one event sponsored by the Guard to pull these families together. Being around others who understood the challenges and stresses was helpful. The Induction Ceremony was not just about celebrating each new Guard member. It was about adding to the extended Guard family.

Arti was met at the door by a handsome and polite young man who introduced himself as Jay. He was decked out in a dress uniform and smiling broadly.

"I was Tee's bunkmate in training. It's tradition for bunkmates to escort their bunkmate's family to their assigned table."

"It's very nice to meet you, Jay. Thank you for the escort," Arti said with a warm smile.

"I've been looking forward to this. Been wanting to

meet the person who is better with a bow than Tee," he said, smiling back at her.

"Tee's been bragging about me," Arti said with a smirk.

"Someone commented that he was the best archer they had ever seen. To which Tee said, 'you haven't seen my mother," Jay said. "He talks about you quite a bit."

Arti smiled and said, "You've often shown up in his letters home. Seems the two of you have become good friends."

Jay winched a little and said sheepishly, "Not at first. But once I got to know him, he won me over."

"He tends to do that. I might be biased, but I think you've made a very good friend," Arti said.

Just then they were stopped by a large intense man who asked in a booming voice, "Jay, is this your mother?"

Jay and Arti were both startled. They turned and looked hard at each other, then broke into laughter. Recovering, Jay said, "No, Sergeant Dee, this is Tee's mother. You're right, we do look related." Dee wouldn't be the only one making that mistake this evening. Both being tall with red hair and pale skin, they stood out. It was an obvious assumption to make.

"My apologies. You must be Arti. Sorry I didn't recognize you. My name is Dee, and I lead recruit training." Dee hesitated a moment and then said, "Your son is unusual to say the least. You must be proud he made it through training."

Arti's smile turned into a frown as she said, "I'm not surprised he made it. I'm proud he's willing to endure the insults and barriers put in his way so that he can dedicate his life to protecting us all."

Dee put up both hands with palms out and, looking embarrassed, said, "I meant no disrespect, Arti. I've gained a lot of respect for Tee. Please enjoy the celebration. You have much to be proud of." And with that, he turned around and walked off.

After Dee had gotten out of hearing, Arti said in a low voice, "I heard all about Dee and his attempts to get Tee to quit."

"It ended up motivating both of us. Dee was obviously trying to get Tee to quit. And you know Tee, that wasn't going to happen. It ended up making Tee the most popular person in training by the end of it. He was the recruit who showed up Dee. To be honest, I wasn't happy when Tee was assigned to be my bunkmate. I knew having a good bunkmate was crucial. I wanted my bunkmate to be physically intimidating. I wanted him to have a mean disposition. Tee just looked so harmless. To everyone's surprise, Tee was the recruit everyone needed to watch out for. I was lucky to get him as a bunkmate."

Arti beamed.

Arriving at the table, Jay turned to a robust couple both with blue eyes and red hair and said, "Mother, Father, this is Tee's mother, Arti."

Jay's mother gave her a warm smile and said, "It's a pleasure to meet you. My name is Pam, and my husband's name is Barin. You just missed Tee. What a nice young man you've got. He stayed with us for the past two weeks. I've been telling Jay to pay attention to Tee. He's been the perfect houseguest."

"You never miss an opportunity for a lecture, Mom," Jay said with an amused look at his mother.

Pam turned to Arti and said, "Here, sit by me. I can tell from Tee that you're someone I'd like to get to know."

Arti wasn't quick to warm up to most people. But Jay's mother was so open, genuine, and warm it was hard not to instantly like her. The table she was seated at had Jay's parents on one side and two other Guard families on the other. One of them included a Wall Archer Arti was familiar with. The organizers had taken care to seat people with similar interests together. Instead of the lonely and emotionally draining experience she had expected, this was turning out to be a pleasant evening.

The ceremony started out with the CGG, narrating a memorial of family members of the recruits who had died protecting Pacifica. It was startling how many of the recruits had members of their immediate families who had lost their lives at the Wall. When he got to Tee's father, he mentioned the lives he had saved helping halt a sudden breach of the Wall. Arti couldn't help it; she hadn't known they would do this. The tears she tried to hold back started to fall. Jay's mother reached over and gently patted her back and whispered, "Thank you for your family's sacrifice, Arti."

What would have felt overly familiar coming from anyone else was strangely comforting. That phrase was a common one. But she could tell Pam meant every word. She had a feeling they would become good friends. Tears came for both mothers when Jay and Tee were called to receive their insignias. Even Jay's father's eyes seemed to shine a bit. The CGG announced that Jay and Tee had the highest bunkmate's score. This meant they would have a thin red stripe running diagonally through their single band insignia. Everyone kept their original Newbie insignia on their uniform, even the CGG. That thin red stripe would be part of their uniforms forever. The Guard was all about achievement as part of a team.

After the presentation, Jay and Tee joined them at their table. Arti gave him a huge hug and held on until Tee said, "Enough, Mom. You can give me more hugs later," to which the table exploded in laughter.

"You look good, son," Arti said quietly, wiping away tears of happiness.

Tee smiled and said, "I feel really good. I'm glad I decided to go ahead with this. It was the hardest thing I've ever done." He gave a grim smile and then said, "I would not have made it if Jay hadn't been assigned my bunkmate."

"He said you've become friends," Arti replied.

Tee smiled. "We have. He's a lot of fun. Reminds me of an intense version of Ansen. How are Ansen and Diana doing?" Tee asked with a wistful look.

"Ansen has been taking on more of the family business responsibilities. He's really matured. And just in time. My brother works too hard and I'm really glad to see Ansen step up and take some of the load off. Diana is Diana. Nothing much has changed other than her constantly asking about you," Arti said.

Nodding, Tee just said, "Good."

Dinner followed, with the recruit instructors serving both the recruits and their families. They were a dangerous-looking group of men, but extremely polite and attentive. After dinner, the crowd started moving around the room, greeting old friends and acquaintances.

Arti smiled as she watched Tee joking around with Jay and some of the other Newbies. A short but sturdy man suddenly appeared and introduced himself with an uncharacteristically soft voice. "Hi, I'm Griff. I don't know if you remember me, Arti."

She looked him in the eyes, studied him for a while

and then said with a small grin, "Of course I do. I remember everyone who almost gets me killed," she said, turning the grin into a warm smile.

Griff chuckled and smiled warmly back. "Perhaps I should go get Nate and have him apologize again." They both laughed softly. "You must be very proud of Tee. He had an especially tough time, and I apologize for putting him in such a difficult situation."

Arti's face took on the intense look he remembered from the Wall and said, "Risk is part of life, it's what enables our survival. I'm very proud that he's willing to step up and do what he can to protect us all."

Arti's face softened, and she continued. "I am appreciative that you looked past his stature and saw his worth. That took an open mind and guts. Your support helped him get to where he is."

Griff nodded and smiled at the compliment, but thought. Oh, Arti. You have that wrong. Those who would love to see me humbled worked very hard to make my experiment fail. Which reminds me, he thought, I have to go find Nate for that drink.

They stood off to the side for a long time, talking and laughing about everything and nothing at all. Tee finally came up and said, "Jay's parents have invited us to their home for a nightcap. Do you want to go?"

"Yes, let's do that. I really like his mother and would like to get to know Jay and his father better."

Arti turned to Griff and said, "It was good to talk to you, Griff. Next time you're in Apple Valley, come to an Archers practice. I am interested in your thoughts on what we can do to better support the Guard."

Griff smiled and said softly, "I would enjoy that, Arti."

As Griff walked away, Tee glanced back at his mother and said, "I didn't know you knew Master Sergeant Ricks."

"I don't, really. We were involved in a firefight at the Wall years and years ago. I was able to support his squad with a difficult retreat and he remembers."

"Oh," said Tee, thinking there was much more to the story. His mother always downplayed what she had done on the Wall. When Tee first saw his mother with Griff, they looked like they were flirting with each other. He almost choked on his beer.

As a teenager, he thought it would be good for her to find someone. Not that he needed a father. But he would eventually be gone and didn't want her to be alone. But Griff? He was a crusty old bastard, and scary as hell. He is the one who got me into the Guard, though. But Mom? He had once bluntly asked her about finding someone.

She had stopped what she was doing, captured him with that intense gaze of hers and said, "Once you're on your own, if I stumble on someone who can hold a candle to your father, it's possible."

And that was all she ever said on the topic.

GUARD EDUCATION

"How was the graduation celebration last week?" Del asked.

"Pretty much like all the others. Caught up with old friends and spent time with the Newbie Guard members and their families," Griff replied.

"I was surprised to see Tee made it," said Del.

"It was a close thing. Dee did everything he could to get Tee to drop out. When that didn't work, he altered the award system to limit his ability to earn points. You have to be in the top fifty by points to be in the Guard," Griff explained.

"Yet somehow he made it," Del replied.

Griff smiled and said, "The somehow is the fun part. Tee ended up out of the top fifty the last week of training. Recruit training has a final test with a large number of points available. We set them loose one at a time on the south side of the Armstrong Reservoir dam. They race around the lake to the north side. Few rules, but one is that you cannot cross over the dam. There is a large variety of trails you can take. Some are direct and fast; others allow you to stay hidden if you're careful. You can challenge anyone you see on the trails to personal combat.

"Guard members act as referees to keep it clean. The loser's race is over and the winner gains points. The strategy for those slow of foot is to win as many personal combat matches as possible and finish. The strategy for the quick is to avoid combat and get to the finish line as soon as possible. There is a large pool of bonus points for the top ten finishers. They divide up the bonus points by the ratio of the difference between the top ten finish times."

"Armstrong Reservoir is huge," Del observed.

"And lots of trails on both sides," Griff said. "We place pickets along some of the trails so you can't just run the whole way. If you miss a picket, you're out. It's usually the evening of the second day before the first recruit finishes. This year, Tee finished in just over an hour."

"Impossible. It's easily twenty miles around the lake," Del said.

"Yeah, but it's only two miles across. Dee wasn't aware that Tee can swim like a fish."

"And you didn't tell him," Del said.

"Guilty." Griff beamed, and they both chuckled.

"Well, I'm glad he made it. I'm guessing he'll be on an officer's track," said Del.

"Ticks all the boxes. He earned respect from the other recruits and the instructors. Toward the end of training, everyone was rooting for him. Even Dee came around," Griff explained.

"Before we get started discussing this year's education plan, I have a question. While I credit the Guard with more common sense than to offer it, why aren't you an officer?" Del asked with a serious look on his face.

"I joined the Guard to fight. Not point the way to battle." Griff scoffed.

Del laughed. "They do a bit more than that. And the lower-level officers do fight."

"Officers start out standing near the battle and pointing. Then they promote you away from the battle to sit down and point some more. It's just not the same."

Del smiled and asked, "So, if you don't want to be an officer, why are you the one defining class requirements for the officers?"

"Because I'm stupid," Griff replied.

"Come now, there's a reason," Del pressed.

"The CGG told me I got this job because I'm opinionated and irritating," Griff said.

"I'm sure that part is true," Del said with an amused expression. "But stupid, you're not. What's the real reason?"

Griff sighed, and with a thoughtful expression said, "Command doesn't see the need for expanding knowledge of warfare outside our current defensive strategy at the Wall and on the cliff forts surrounding the peninsula. We are extremely vulnerable if the GEMs break past the Wall. Once they do, they can threaten the Landfall Dam. We have to be prepared for a retreat to the Eureka Dam. Then, if it all goes to hell, a phased plan to evacuate all the way to the Apple Lakes region. Successfully managing a retreat is difficult.

"Decisions must be made quickly, and they must be the right decisions. Less important, but still critical in my opinion, is that we aren't prepared to go on the offensive. Sure, we make limited forays below the Wall, but it's not the same thing as a concentrated, well-managed offensive campaign with contingencies. While that might seem crazy now, if there is an opportunity to deal them a serious blow, we should be prepared to take advantage of it."

Del was secretly delighted with this answer and was careful not to show his enthusiasm. An opportunity to train officers for broader military roles and expose them to the technology of the past was urgently needed. I can't tell Griff why we need this, but he's just given me the excuse for a course of study that could sneak some of that in.

"Okay, that actually makes sense. Would you like me to propose something?" Del offered with a bland voice.

"That's why I'm here," Griff replied.

"You realize this is a pretty big change from what we've been doing," Del said.

"Yeah, but it can't look like we're making a big departure from the past. We have to slip this past the CGG."

"Off the top of my head, it sounds like a program that reviews military history, strategy, and weapon systems. We can test their ability to respond to new military objectives with war games."

Griff stared back at him a bit confused and said, "I'm not trying to turn them into history students."

Del leaned forward and said, "If you want them to think outside the current strategy, you need to broaden and deepen their education. If retreat planning is important, we can focus on understanding retreats in the past that were well executed. We can compare them with those that were disasters. Many times, they were both. Dunkirk on old Earth is an example of disaster being turned into success. To understand the decisions that were made, you have to understand the era's technical capabilities. We can specifically design one of the war games as a sudden retreat from the Wall to Eureka Valley and then continuing on to Apple Lakes under various conditions."

"That sounds good to me, but we don't have lots of study time with all their other responsibilities," Griff countered.

"We can phase in the education and have it increment based on rank level. That way, we spread it out over time. Go more in depth for the higher ranks, or those with high potential for promotion. You'll have to convince them that newly promoted officers need a special set of classes in addition to the ongoing education we already do. You guys like to haze Newbies and newly promoted officers. Make it sound like they are paying their dues or some such BS."

Griff thought for a bit. With concern on his face, he said, "When can I see the details?"

"Tomorrow afternoon if you buy me dinner tonight," Del said.

"Done, but you're buying the drinks. A real beer this time!" Griff said sternly.

CHAPTER 18

BLUE HERON TAVERN

Tee and Jay's lives fell into a routine. They each worked hard at training five days a week and hung out with Guard Newbies from their recruit class most nights below the dam. On weekends, Jay and Tee would hike up to Landfall City and spend Friday and Saturday nights there. The Phillips embraced Tee like he was one of the family. He had his own bedroom. When he was ready to do his university classes, they insisted he stay with them. Tee, Quinn, and Hestie replaced Friday night bonfires with dinner and drinks at one of the taverns in the center of town. Jay was usually at home with his parents and brothers or hanging out with his old school friends. Tee thought he might have a girlfriend, but didn't talk about her.

One Friday evening Jay said, "Tee, can I come and meet Quinn and Hestie?" I've met their parents and the rest of your friends in Apple Valley but not them yet."

"Absolutely," Tee said with enthusiasm. "They've asked lots of questions about you, and I know they want to meet you." He hesitated, smiled, and said, "How are you going to explain that shiner?"

Jay narrowed his eyes and gave Tee a look that said back off, "I walked into a door, Tee."

Tee was unconvinced, but decided they each had their

secrets, so perhaps he should just let it go. It was drizzling as they quickly walked to the Blue Heron Tavern, trying not to get too wet. Tee turned to Jay and said, "One word of warning. Quinn doesn't have any tact whatsoever. He is brilliant. But whatever part of the brain manages social interactions is busy doing something else. If he says something odd, or even wildly insulting, just ignore it. He is completely genuine, harmless, and doesn't have a mean bone in his body."

"He's like his mom, then," Jay said.

"Exactly. Except a happier version," Tee explained, smiling.

"No problem. His mom told me with a straight face at the bonfire that personal hygiene was important for good health," Jay said smiling, "We really should have bathed after we got back from hunting, Tee."

Tee chuckled and said, "Yeah, ran out of time. But I'll remember to plan better next time."

They walked into the tavern and spied Quinn and Hestie in a back booth. Tee made introductions, and they ordered drinks.

"Can I try a sip of whatever that is you're drinking? I've never seen anything with that color before," Jay said.

"Sure," Tee said.

Jay tentatively tried a sip, screwed up his face, and said, "Yuk. A drink shouldn't taste like that. Is this an Apple Valley thing? You people do the most disgusting stuff."

Tee grinned, turned toward Quinn and Hestie and said, "He's referring to our hunting trip. I took the big tough city boy with me to Apple Valley. He almost puked while I was dressing the deer we shot."

"You shot, and then talked me into carrying most of

it back."

"You had to earn your meal somehow. Just wasting my time otherwise," Tee said, earning a knowing look from Jay.

"You are never going to let that go, are you?" Jay said with an affected grimace.

"Not likely," said Tee with a grin.

"I did like the bonfire at the beach and roasting venison over the fire," Jay said.

"Did you meet everyone?" Quinn asked.

"I met Ansen, Diana, their parents, their brothers and sisters, and Grammy. Oh, and your parents were there too," Jay said, "It was quite the party."

"Did Grammy get you off to the side and extract your secrets?" Hestie asked with a warm smile.

"I like Grammy," Jay said enthusiastically, "And we did have a long talk." Jay hesitated and then confessed sheepishly, "Which included some advice." Everyone broke into raucous laughter.

"I can't believe what I ended up telling her," Jay said, shaking his head to even more laughter.

"You have to watch Grammy," Tee said. "Her advice tends to get repeated more and more firmly until she's satisfied you've followed it."

"It means she likes you, Jay," said Hestie. "It means you're officially part of the group," she added warmly.

Tee turned to Hestie and said, "How are your medical classes going?"

"Well, we've been dissecting, so I'm not sure it's a good topic just before dinner," Hestie said softly, then glanced over at Jay and gave him a shy grin.

Tee chuckled and said, "Wouldn't want anybody to get queasy."

Jay narrowed his eyes at Tee and said, "Okay, little man. Enough!" Then he looked at Hestie and said with interest, "What are you studying?"

"It's mostly basic biology and human anatomy. My mom's a doctor and I've been helping her with patients for a while. I know most of it already. I'm not sure if I want to be a doctor like my mom or something else. I'm also studying genetics, which I love and want to explore more deeply. I know I want to help people, so I'm trying to figure out what that means," Hestie said.

As Jay and Hestie continued their conversation, Tee turned to Quinn and said, "How is the mad scientist training going?"

"It's wonderful having access to the whole library and Professor Dacy's lab. It's like going to heaven. I was worried I would get stuck in lower-level classes for a few years, but they let me test out," Quinn said with enthusiasm.

Quinn being worried about anything was a significant event. Must have been a full-blown crisis. Tee thought wryly. "So, what did you test out of, Quinn?"

"They gave me all the credits for undergraduate degrees in mathematics, physics, chemistry, and mechanical engineering. I still have to take the required courses in history, English, biology, debate, and a special class in social awareness before I get those degrees," Quinn said casually.

Tee was stunned. He knew Quinn was smart, but it was hard to believe he had tested out of all the non-biology science and technology classes the university had to offer. He smiled about the "special class in social awareness." He bet the professors had scrambled trying to figure out how to deal with Quinn. What they would discover was that Quinn was exactly what he appeared to be. Crazy about science. Kind to everyone. No hidden agendas. And no tact whatsoever. Quinn told the truth without the limitation of worrying how it would affect others. He was a wildly enthusiastic and visibly happy version of his mother.

"So, if you tested out of all those classes, what do they have you studying?" Tee asked.

Quinn's face suddenly became guarded. He collected himself and tentatively said, "They have me doing special projects that involve reviewing incomplete archives from long ago. I'm being asked to reverse engineer what is missing in the archives."

Tee's face clouded. He knew Quinn really well. His explanation sounded like something he had memorized. Quinn was hiding something. Tee was sure he hadn't seen Quinn try to do this since they were little kids. He was bad at it then, and he is bad at it now. Well, the Guard has its secrets too and Tee didn't want to stress Quinn out by asking more questions about his 'special projects'.

"You mentioned Professor Dacy's lab. What does he have in it?"

"Everything!" Quinn burst out in excitement. He went on and on about the measurement equipment, lab supplies, reference materials, and notebooks from previous special projects. Tee sat, nodding his head, understanding some of it, but just letting Quinn rattle on and on. Much of it was interesting, and it gave him pleasure to watch his old friend be so excited about what he was doing with his life. They both had blessings. Tee was thankful for his, and for Quinn's.

As Quinn droned on and on, Tee stole a glance over to Jay and Hestie. They were both leaning in toward one another slightly and talking intently, eyes locked. Well, that's interesting, thought Tee. A good match. While Jay was a monster in the Guard, he had a soft side he wasn't afraid to show once he trusted you. Hestie was a lot like Jay's mother in temperament and where Tee thought Jay's soft side came from.

Quinn suddenly said something that piqued his interest. "They have electrical equipment in the lab?" Tee asked to confirm what he thought he heard.

Quinn froze, looked down at the table, looked up, and said, "Some really basic experimental stuff."

"Oh interesting, I bet that's fun," said Tee, knowing Quinn had just lied to him. He was stunned by that realization and his interest peaked.

"Yes, it is," said Quinn as his face turned a light shade of red.

Just then, Jay saved the day by saying, "Tee. Hestie wants to know what training we're both doing. I explained what they have me doing, but you should explain yours."

"I haven't started it yet, but I'm scheduled to take a bunch of history courses focused on military strategy. It's organized by maneuver. For instance, one of the first classes is dedicated to retreat planning and execution. It reviews significant failures and successes in the past when an army has had to retreat. I was told I'm going to have to understand military technology for each era examined. The idea being that to understand why certain choices were made, you have to have the full context of the situation. When I get to that point, I'm hoping Quinn can help me," Tee said, stealing a glance at Quinn as he sat stone faced. Gotcha, thought Tee. He's studying something along the lines of what they have me signed up for.

"What will be fun are the war games we get to play once the class has finished. It's coordinated with Jay's training. We will be part of a team. We are given starting conditions and have to quickly plan and execute a retreat. It's interactive with Guard officers, non-coms, and university staff, giving us situational updates as we work through the exercise. Should be fun," Tee said.

"Sounds like being on the losing team in capture-the-flag," Hestie said.

Tee hesitated, thinking about Hestie's observation, and said, "That's a good analogy. It's like we're moving the flag to somewhere we can protect it," Tee said thoughtfully.

The conversation continued briskly for quite some time and then started to slow as it got late. Tee, reading the room, finally said, "Well, Jay and I better go. We have physical training that starts early and goes all day."

As they said their goodbyes, Hestie turned to Jay and said, "I hope you can join us again, Jay. I enjoyed talking to you."

Jay smiled warmly and said, "Goodnight, Hestie, I'm sure I'll come with Tee again one of these nights."

They walked back toward Jay's home in silence for a while. Jay broke the silence with, "I wouldn't mind coming along next week if it's okay with you."

"You're always welcome, Jay. Both Hestie and Quinn like you, and it was fun tonight," Tee said.

"They both seem pretty smart," Jay offered.

"That's the understatement of the year," Tee said,

amused.

"Does Hestie have a boyfriend?" Jay asked tentatively.

"Is that your way of asking me if I'm interested in her?" Tee said in an amused tone.

"Yeah, that, and whether there is anyone else," Jay said.

"The answer to both is no, unless there is someone I don't know about. And I doubt that because she would tell me. I love Hestie. But not like that. She and Quinn grew up next door, and she's like a sister to me. One I care deeply about, so don't you dare hurt her," Tee said with his voice getting slightly strained.

"You know me better than that," Jay said, obviously more than a little offended.

Tee stopped, looked at Jay, sighed and said, "I'm sorry I said that. I do know who you are. Hestie means a lot to me. You won't find a nicer person, or one who cares as much about others as she does," Tee said, which seemed to satisfy Jay.

They continued to walk in silence until Jay said, "You need to work on getting that chip off your shoulder. You have no reason to be suspicious, defiant, or worry like you do."

Only a true friend would take the risk of saying something like that, Tee thought. Jay was right, and he needed to stop. "You're right, Jay, I'll work on it."

And with that admission, they both relaxed and retreated to their own thoughts.

Tee's thoughts turned back to the evening. He knew when Hestie had gone from interesting to exciting for Jay. Quinn said something socially unacceptable and then left to go to the men's room. Jay had looked questioningly in Hestie's direction as she watched Quinn walk away. With fondness in her voice, she said, "The world would be a better place if everyone could just say what they think without anyone taking offense or judging them." Jay's gaze went from questioning to thoughtfulness until Hestie turned toward him, and he quickly looked away. They really would make a great couple.

CHAPTER 19

GLORIA

Hestie thought one of the best things her mother had done for her children was to show them how to learn. It wasn't enough to sit in a classroom and follow a carefully laid out plan of study. It was about being curious and following that curiosity wherever it took you. With their mother's help, Hestie and her brother had been involved in self-study at the university level since primary school. Quinn had tested out of his lower-level classes so he could take on challenging work.

Hestie had taken a different path. She kept hidden what she already knew. This allowed her to breeze through her lower-level biology and anatomy classes, giving her plenty of time to delve deeply into topics that interested and challenged her. The one that most absorbed her was studying the intricate blueprint and construction plan of life. DNA was the blueprint. The construction plan was a complex set of organic and chemical signals that determined when and how that blueprint was executed.

Evolution was driven by the dance of random changes to both the blueprint and the construction plan. Sometimes these changes were beneficial and carried forward. Sometimes they were detrimental and resulted in a dead end. She was fascinated by the incredible intelligence behind all of it. She was determined to learn as much as she could. The fact they had never found complex life outside of that originating on Earth was mind-boggling. In addition to making terraforming easier, it fed the bright fires of theological debate. Atheists used this fact to claim that the low probability of complex life forming naturally was verified by how rare it was. Believers in an intelligent creator used that same knowledge to claim it proved God uniquely created everything, just as the ancient texts claimed.

Hestie thought it was silly to use science to prove or disprove God's existence. Both camps' beliefs were faith based. Only an agnostic was devoid of faith. Hestie had a strong faith in God, goodness, and the obligation to fight evil. Grammy had instilled that early on and the more she knew, the more that strength grew.

It was unfortunate that studying genetics was considered suspicious. The horrible wars and pogroms that resulted from humankind experimenting with artificial evolution made it a touchy topic even two millennia later. The one thing that could automatically get you thrown out of the university, and perhaps into jail, was to attempt to artificially alter any of the drivers of life.

Hybridization was acceptable since it simply favored beneficial characteristics already present. Nothing was invented or created. Change by direct manipulation was the most heinous crime imaginable. The reality of GEMs was all the evidence one needed to understand the danger.

Given the fear and anger surrounding the topic, Hestie had decided at a young age to keep her talents hidden. She had an ability to read and understand this complex dance. What genes described. Why some turned on and some turned off. How cell specialization was generated. It scared her to realize she had the ability to design genetic changes to achieve a desired outcome. It scared her further when she realized she had a deeper understanding of these mechanisms than her mother did. Her mother was thought to be the smartest person on the planet.

It was embarrassing to think she knew more than her mother, at least in that one area. Perhaps she was arrogant. Maybe she didn't really understand as much as she thought she did. Hestie, by nature, was most comfortable in the background. It was an easy decision to hide her gift.

"Hestie, you need to come up for air," Gloria said with an affected frown, which transformed into a smile once she had her attention.

"Sorry Gloria. I just get so absorbed in this stuff sometimes." Gloria was Hestie's new friend. Gloria was extremely attractive. It was odd walking around with her since men of all ages would be staring at her while trying to look like they weren't. They would engage Hestie in conversation with the obvious end goal of meeting Gloria. That part of the friendship was uncomfortable. They had met in the university dining hall one night when Gloria bumped into her.

After both taking turns taking the blame and apologizing profusely, they laughed and eventually sat down and had dinner together. Since then, they had started studying together in the library most evenings. Gloria was in her biology class, so Hestie would help her from time to time. While Gloria wasn't Diana, she was beginning to be someone she could call a friend.

"I don't understand how you can get anything out of looking at pages and pages of A's, C's, G's, and T's. I know that has to have something to do with DNA. Isn't it undecipherable to just look at the letters?" Gloria said.

Hestie had to be more careful with her private studies in public like this. Gloria was anything but stupid. And now she was suspicious. She hadn't even noticed Gloria sitting down across from her. "You're right, it's a waste of time trying to make sense out of it," Hestie said as her eyes adjusted from her work to her friend.

"You need to get out more, girl. A friend of mine saw you studying with me the other day and he is very interested in meeting you, very interested. He's a nice guy and is having a small party Friday night. Do you want to go with me?"

"I've already got plans for Friday, Gloria. My brother and I are meeting up with Tee. I've told you about him before. He was our next-door neighbor growing up in Apple Valley. I've known him all my life. He's in the Guard and taking military history classes at the university this semester." To say nothing of the fact that Jay would be there, Hestie thought.

Jay had been on her mind a lot lately. Meeting up on Friday nights had become a regular thing and the more she got to know him, the more she liked him. He was kind, gentle, witty, and intelligent. The knowledge he was capable of protecting her against just about anything was also a little exciting. The fact she thought he was the most attractive man she had ever seen didn't hurt, either.

Better yet, he didn't seem to know how handsome he was. Best of all was that he was solidly, emotionally secure. He didn't need her help to understand himself. Didn't need a shoulder to lean on. They could just lean together. They had met up a couple of times on Saturdays. He had been the perfect gentleman every time. No pressure for anything physical, which she especially appreciated, given how physically imposing he was. She was starting to think she was going to have to be the one to initiate things if it went any further. She felt valued, appreciated, happy, and safe around Jay. She was in danger of falling in love and wasn't fighting it.

"Either you don't like men or you're hiding a boyfriend, Hestie. You've avoided every attempt I've made to introduce you. The only other thing I can think of is that you don't like my company," Gloria said with a rare frown, inviting disagreement with her last comment.

Hestie stared at her for a few moments, wondering where to go with this. There was something different about Gloria, and she couldn't figure out what it was. Of course, she was the last one who should be critical of anyone being 'unusual.' Her entire family was strange. Perhaps she was reluctant to talk about Jay because she was a little afraid of how serious it was becoming. Deciding to open up, she said, "Tee has a friend from the Guard that I've been spending time with. I'm not someone who sees more than one guy at a time. It just doesn't seem right for you to introduce me to anyone right now."

"Ohhh!" Gloria said, clapping her hands together, obviously delighted with the news. "Tell me everything."

Hestie smiled thinking about Jay and proceeded to list his attributes, getting enthusiastic as she warmed up to the idea of sharing this with Gloria. When she said he was raised in the Landfall City, Gloria stopped her and said, "What's his name?"

"Jay Phillips," Hestie responded, smiling.

Gloria just stared back at Hestie with shock showing clearly on her face. As the shocked look turned into concern, she said, "I hate to be the one to tell you this, but Jay Phillips is not a good guy. I went to school with him. He's beautiful, and he's charming. I'll give him that.

But he's the worst kind of bully. He randomly targets popular boys and stalks them until they are alone and then beats them up. I heard he got caught by the friends of one of his intended targets a few weeks ago and was beaten badly. I spied him in town with a black eye just after that. It delighted almost everyone he went to school with. Worse, he takes advantage of girls and laughs about it later. The only thing he wants is their virginity."

Hestie was stunned speechless. She just stared back at Gloria, not knowing what to say. She finally looked down, gathered her books, and got up to leave.

"Don't run away, Hestie. I'm here for you. I'm sorry, but it's kinder to warn you about what type of man you're seeing. I just couldn't stay silent."

Tears were spilling from her eyes as she turned away and almost ran from the library. How could she have been such a fool? Girl from Apple Valley taken advantage of by the big city boy. She felt completely humiliated as she ducked her head and walked out into the rainy streets of the capital.

A few days later, it was Friday evening. Hestie was walking along crowded streets to meet Tee, Quinn, and Jay at the Blue Heron Tavern. It was a popular medium-sized place to have dinner and drinks located in the center of the city. It was frequented by a wide mix of people and had a rustic feel to it that reminded Hestie of The Apple Lakes Inn. The familiar atmosphere was likely why Tee originally suggested it.

She had spent two days berating herself for being fooled and almost told Quinn she was skipping Friday night. Then she realized the story didn't add up. First of all, she had high confidence in Tee's ability to read people. He would not be friends with a bully or someone who treated women badly. Of that, she was sure. He would certainly not be okay with someone he didn't trust dating her.

She smiled, thinking about the one kiss they had shared a few years ago. It was a quick one. They had immediately pulled away from each other and broke out laughing. Ansen had been pushing the idea that they should be a couple and that influenced them both. It was their secret. Having anyone else know would just cause embarrassment and confusion. Tee was her other brother. She was his sister. They loved each other. He was as close to her as any family member could be. He was the brother she didn't need to explain to others. The one she could open up to and would understand.

Could Tee have been fooled about Jay's true nature? That was certainly possible. Tee tended to believe in the best in people. But it seemed unlikely that Jay could have fooled them both. While she wasn't perfect, everyone said her ability to read people was extraordinary. All of her senses, all of her intuition, said that Jay was simply what he appeared to be. But she needed to confront him. Grammy always said it's better to fess up first to yourself and then everyone else in matters of the heart.

She smiled at the thought of Grammy wearing her stern face while lecturing all of them. Grammy's advice was always helpful if you bothered to follow it. When Hestie entered the tavern, Tee, Quinn, and Jay were already there.

She walked up to the table, skipped her normal greetings, looked directly at Jay, and said, "Jay, there is something I'd like to talk to you about. Can we go to another table?"

Well, that certainly caused an emotional upheaval for

both Jay and Tee. Her empathy was so strong that their reaction caused a jolt of emotional pain for her. It was not in her nature to be blunt. She could feel the waves of anxiety flowing out from both of them. Quinn, of course, was oblivious. She didn't need to worry about him for now. Tee's face quickly went from anxious to throwing a questioning look at Jay. Perhaps there is something to what Gloria told her after all, she thought, with a sinking feeling in her gut.

"Sure," said Jay in a soft voice and got up from the table. He followed her over to a private table in the corner and sat down.

"What's this all about?" he asked, worry written all over him. Jay was an observant man, something she liked about him.

"You told me a few weeks ago that I could ask you anything. Can I?" Hestie said with a flat and slightly stern expression.

"Yes, you can ask me anything," Jay said, leaning back from the table a bit, concern clearly growing.

"The day we met, your face was bruised. Tee was teasing you about how that happened. He clearly did not believe your story. How did your face get bruised?"

Jay's face showed surprise and confusion. He hesitated, then said, "Not sure why it matters to you, but I'll tell you if you promise to keep it a secret from Tee."

Hestie's eyebrows narrowed with suspicion. She hesitated a few moments and then said, "I won't promise that. If there is something going on that Tee ought to know, I'm going to tell him. He's family to me."

Jay pondered that for a minute, clearly concerned with the direction of the conversation. Then he took a deep breath and said, "You clearly don't trust me for some reason. But that doesn't mean I don't trust you. I'll tell you what happened, and you can decide whether to tell him or not." Hestie nodded for him to continue and her features softened just a bit.

"Tee had a horrible time in recruit training. It's still hard for me to believe anyone could take that kind of abuse and just keep going. After you get to know Tee, you learn to expect uncompromising bullheadedness out of him. Since you've known him your whole life, I'm sure you're not surprised."

Hestie nodded at that, and the corners of her mouth bent up a fraction. "Tee is a force of nature at times."

Encouraged, Jay continued. "If you know that you also know how much be berates himself if he has to rely on anyone for protection. Nothing worse for Tee than not being able to personally take care of his own problems."

Hestie thought about this and then said, "You're right. It's stupid, but he hates having to rely on anyone. So, what happened?"

"You know that Tee and I are Newbies." Hestie nodded to show she understood. "We aren't considered full Guard members until we complete our training. That means we get some good-natured ribbing when we run into the various Guard units. The night before we met, I was at a bar near the Wall with a guy named Kale having a few beers. Kale was in the same recruit class as Tee and I. He was horrible to Tee throughout most of our training. Then he completely turned around and became one of Tee's biggest supporters. We're all good friends now.

"Anyway, five members of Scout Team 2 came into the bar, noticed us, and started with the common insults thrown at Newbies. We laughed along with them at the first few jibes and then ignored them. They were a little drunk, and ignoring them made them angry. That's when the largest of them asked if we knew the midget who had just graduated. We continued to ignore them, so he walked over to Kale, poked him in the chest, and said, 'I'm talking to you, Newbie.'

Kale took a step back, looked him up and down and said, 'His name is Tee, and he's a better man than you are.' The next thing I knew, Kale and I were in a brawl with all five of them. The Guard police showed up, and we spent the night locked up."

"Were you hurt?" Hestie asked, clearly concerned.

"Not really. But I do know that Scout Team 2 has readjusted their opinion of the latest Newbie class," he said with a self-satisfied smile. "The best part was when Master Sergeant Ricks showed up the next morning. He told Scout Team 2 in front of their staff sergeant that they were lucky Tee wasn't with us. He's tougher than either one of these guys, pointing his thumb over at us.

"Kale and I nodded in agreement at that. He told all of us he doesn't want to hear this being discussed. He told us we were an embarrassment to the Guard. Then he slowly looked around the room, looked all of us in the eye, and said he would personally make life a living hell for anyone who talks about the incident or doesn't treat other Guard members like brothers going forward."

"So, you're under orders not to talk about it and you're also worried Tee will feel bad about himself if he knows," Hestie said.

"That's about it," Jay responded.

Hestie considered this for a few moments and said softly, "I won't say anything, Jay. I don't want to get you in trouble. I agree there is no reason for Tee to know."

Jay looked at her suspiciously and then asked, "What is this really all about?"

"One more question," Hestie said with an intense look back in place. "Are you trying to trick me into giving you my virginity?"

"What?" exploded out of him loudly enough that it caused people at the tables nearby to turn and look at them. Even Quinn turned around with a rare look of concern on his face. Jay looked at her sternly for a while and whispered, "No. I'll only ask that of my wife on our wedding night."

Although she saw he was clearly offended, Hestie relaxed. There was no doubt in her mind he was telling the truth. She was surprised how important this was to her. There would be so much more than just humiliation if the accusations had been true. Gloria was lying about all of it. But why?

"I'm truly sorry, Jay. I really am. I was told some things about you that were just horrible. It was so bad I wasn't able to just trust my instincts and ignore it." A moment passed and then she said, "Do you know Gloria Binder?"

Jay's eyebrows crashed together. He turned a bright shade of red and was obviously working hard to keep his anger in check. "Yes," he bit off. "We were dating at school and then for a brief time after I came back from recruit training. We broke up before you and I met."

"Why did you break up?" Hestie asked.

Jay considered this for a few moments and then said, "Let's just say our ethics and morals weren't in alignment."

Hestie appreciated that Jay didn't say anything more

than that. Clearly, something disturbing happened. She wasn't going to ask him about it. Now she had a different problem. She had broken trust with Jay. She should have just trusted him. Told him about the accusations and let him explain.

"Jay, I am truly sorry. I should have come straight to you with what had been said. I know deep down that you're trustworthy. I won't make that mistake again."

Jay just glared back at her for an uncomfortable minute. Then he said in a stern voice, "I have a serious question for you."

Hestie's insides roiled. If her mistake meant he wasn't interested in her anymore, it would be terrible. She was frightened by how important he had become to her. Taking a shallow breath, she nodded for him to continue.

Jay's frown grew even deeper, and he said, "How do I know this isn't some elaborate plan to take *my* virginity?"

Hestie just stared at him dumbly for a few moments, her brain not able to make sense of what she had just heard. Then she burst into laughter, rocking slightly back and forth, trying to gain control. Jay was smiling broadly and chuckling at the spectacle, clearly pleased with himself. She got up, went around to the other side, jumped in his lap, and gave him a huge hug.

"Thank you, Jay," she said softly into his ear. "I really am sorry." Then, turning around, she saw Tee and Quinn staring at them. "We should probably go over and save the evening. Tee has been stealing anxious glances at us the whole time."

Later that evening, after dropping the twins off at their dorm rooms, Tee and Jay were walking back to Jay's house and Tee asked, "Everything okay with you and Hestie?"

"Yeah, just boyfriend girlfriend stuff," Jay said.

Tee smiled and said with a touch of sarcasm, "So it's official, the two of you like each other."

"Yes we do, smartass," Jay replied.

Tee put his hand on Jay's shoulder and with an honest and earnest expression said, "Jay, I couldn't be happier for you, or for Hestie."

Jay was touched. He remembered their first conversation about Hestie and Tee's initial concern with him being interested in her. Tee was rarely serious about these sorts of things, which made it all the more genuine. An affected frown was on Jay's face and turning the tables on Tee, he said, "You Apple Valley people have trust issues." Seeing the confused, questioning look he expected, he turned away and hid a smile. Let him sort that one out, he thought. They continued their walk to Jay's house in silence

158

CHAPTER 20

DIANA'S HUNT

Diana was getting more and more frustrated with Ansen. Ansen decided he would go hunting with her because he thought it was dangerous for her to be in the woods alone. This was reasonable on the surface. It was rare, but there were panthers and bears who had been known to attack people. Not that she couldn't take care of herself. But it did sound nice to hunt with someone again.

Ansen was LOUD. He walked loudly. He breathed loudly. He would not stop talking. She enjoyed Ansen's banter most of the time. He had an unusual way of looking at life, which was entertaining and very funny. But damn it, this was a hunt, not a party at the beach. She finally decided it was her own fault. Ansen was always loud, so why should this be any different? So, she came up with a plan.

"Let's walk up to the beach lookout and see the guys," Diana said.

"So, you going to give up on hunting with me?" Ansen asked suspiciously.

Diana rolled her eyes upward and said, "Yes! Let's go see the guys and you can hang out with them. That way, you can stop pretending to enjoy the woods while I go hunting in peace for a couple of hours."

Ansen looked a little hurt and said, "Am I that bad?"

Diana smiled and said, "The worst! You are unbelievably loud. You're scaring all the game away."

"Fair enough," Ansen said.

Then, to Diana's amazement, he stopped talking. Diana really missed hunting with Tee. He had been gone for almost six months now and only came back once in all that time. He had his friend Jay from the Guard with him and the two of them had gone hunting. Diana wasn't invited. Tee and Diana had been roaming the woods together since they were old enough to be allowed to wander off. The woods relaxed her. She really liked supplying fresh meat for family and friends.

Being honest with herself, she had to admit she just plain missed Tee. It wasn't just the hunting trips. It was hard to be completely honest with herself, but Tee leaving left a hole. She could feel it in the pit of her stomach. Hunting just made the pain more pronounced. She adored Ansen. He was kind, witty, funny, and trustworthy. But she loved Tee. There, she admitted it. She knew deep down it was true. She had been in denial. He was not as funny or entertaining as Ansen, but you could have deep, soulful conversations with him. He understood her like no one else.

When he was around, she was simply at peace. He was short and slender, shorter than she was. But he always seemed to be the largest person around when there was a crisis or threat of some kind. She might have been surprised when he was chosen for the Guard. Everyone was, including him. But she wasn't shocked. How did I get myself into this situation, she thought. Everyone, including Ansen, thinks we'll marry this year.

Why did I run away from Tee for so long? Why were those feelings so scary? Well, some serious thinking to do and the woods have always been the best place for that.

"How do you think Quinn, Hestie, and Tee are doing?" Diana asked. She figured they might as well talk until they got to the lookout.

Ansen replied, "I haven't heard anything lately. It sucks that all three of them are gone. I miss them even more than I thought I would. But I'm really glad they are all in the capital and see each other regularly." Ansen sighed and then continued. "To be honest, I wanted Tee to get kicked out of recruit training. But he made it to graduation, so he's Guard for life." Diana just nodded in agreement. "I gave him an earful the last time he was up here about Hestie," Ansen said. "She has a heart of gold, loves him to death, and just keeps getting prettier. I do not understand why he doesn't pursue her. She isn't going to be available forever."

Diana spoke up with resignation, "I always dreamed the four of us being close forever. I imagined being on the beach Friday nights with Hestie and I trading kids back and forth while you and Tee trade insults." She smiled a wry and somewhat guilty smile."

Ansen said, "I think he's confused...LOOK OUT!"

They had rounded a curve in the trail and standing in a small clearing were three GEMs looking right at them. The GEMs didn't hesitate. They immediately broke into a run, pulling out wicked looking short swords. Diana didn't hesitate, either. She immediately drew back her already notched arrow and placed it in the throat of the lead GEM. This didn't slow the other two down at all.

A few feet away now, Diana had just enough time to draw a second arrow from the quiver, pull back and let fly. She watched in amazement as the arrow buried itself deeply in the second GEM's left eye socket. He dropped like a stone. She said a quick prayer and silently thanked Arti for all the endless crazy battle scenario drills she used to make them do. She had instinctively avoided their torsos because she didn't have time to decide if they had on armor or not.

Without that training, she would be dead or at the mercy of the GEMs. And the GEMs had no mercy. She quickly turned and saw that Ansen was wounded and barely holding the last GEM off. He was using a tree as a shield of sorts, but it was clear he wouldn't be able to hold him off for long with just his knife. Diana took another arrow and pulled back. She slowly circled the fight, looking for an opening.

There was a lot of quick movement by both of them that was hard to predict. If she missed, she would hit Ansen. Again, she heard Arti in her head telling her to concentrate, focus on getting a good shot, don't wait for the perfect shot. She let go, and the arrow grazed Ansen's forearm before burying itself in the GEM's side just below the vest and into the rib cage. This distracted the GEM enough that Ansen was able to step in close and drive his knife deep into the creature's chest.

Diana notched another arrow and looked around wildly. Two of the GEMs were quite dead. The one with the arrow in his neck was noisily bleeding out, so no threat there. The three GEMs had yelled loudly when they saw Diana and Ansen, so she believed others must be nearby. Ansen seemed to be in shock, but his wound wasn't serious enough to worry about it now.

"We have to run back to Apple Lake Ansen," Diana said.

"Shouldn't we rouse the guys at the lookout instead?" Ansen countered.

"They're dead Ansen. The only way those GEMs are here is by scaling the beach cliff. They must have surprised the lookout." Diana realized Ansen was not thinking clearly. So, she grabbed his shirt, gave him a pull back down the trail and broke into a run, hoping he would follow.

After they had been running for several minutes, her panicked mind settled down. She wondered if they should both run back to Apple Lake. There was another lookout just a bit further south, about twenty minutes or so off this main trail. The cliff below this lookout had no beach. Large waves pounded directly into the sheer granite wall, so very unlikely it had been directly assaulted.

Since they had surprised the scouts fairly close to the beach lookout, she hoped the GEMs weren't there yet. The lookout was there for one reason: a signal fire could be seen from Apple Lake and the next signal fire station in Eureka Valley below the falls. The quickest way to get a response team was to get that signal fire lit. The only problem was that it was a dead-end trail. If GEMs were following, they would come up that trail and trap them at the lookout.

"Ansen, you keep going down the trail to Apple Lake and report to Major Richards. I'm going to light the southern cliff top signal fire. We have to make sure this invasion is known all the way to the capital as soon as possible."

"No, Diana!" Ansen yelled with a wild-eyed expression, "I am not leaving you!" He grabbed her arm tightly, pulling her away from the branched trail to the cliff top lookout and down the trail to Apple Lake.

Diana calmed herself, stopped, and with her free hand slapped him hard, saying, "Get ahold of yourself! This isn't about you and me. It's about everyone in Pacifica. We have to split up to give a better chance of getting the news out." Ansen's expression changed from wild-eyed to shocked. He took a deep breath and said, "You're right, I'm sorry. Just please make sure you live. I will never forgive you if you don't." Even at the worst of times, Ansen was trying to joke. It fell flat.

Diana stopped running as she approached the lookout. She left the trail and carefully crept through the woods toward the clearing at the top of the cliff. She saw the huge stack of wood comprising the signal. She stopped, listened, and looked for GEMs. The two lookouts who were supposed to be there seemed to be missing. It was completely silent, with no one in sight. The small fire that was supposed to always be going was cold. Luckily, her mother insisted she take flint and steel with her when she went hunting. "You never know when you might get stuck out there for the night and a fire can come in handy," her mother had said.

Diana took a deep breath and shaved off some chips. With time, she got a small ember going. Then some smaller pieces of wood and was finally able to get the end of a dead tree branch glowing. She got up quickly, sticking the burning branch into the signal firewood stack, and WHOOSH the whole thing exploded. She fell back on her butt, smelling burned hair. She had forgotten the signal firewood was soaked in a flammable liquid just for this purpose. Quinn would know exactly what. Right down to the chemical bonding diagram.

She smiled and realized she was a bit loopy thinking about Quinn's weird store of knowledge at a time like this. She needed to focus. Checking herself over, she wasn't injured. She thought her hair was singed and worried her eyebrows might be gone.

"Now is not the time to worry about how pretty you are, Diana," she said out loud with a nervous laugh.

Gazing out to sea, she saw three large vessels on the very edge of the horizon that seemed to be heading north of the cliff lookout and toward the beach. Given the strong headwinds and choppy seas, it was going to take a while. She was terrified of what it would mean if hundreds or thousands of GEMs were able to scale the cliff and get entrenched in the upper east valley. She shuttered as she thought back to the demonic vicious smiles of the GEMs.

Her immediate problem, however, was she had just advertised to the GEMs where they could find her. She shouldn't go back down the trail and waiting by the signal fire seemed incredibly stupid. Walking around, she carefully studied the perimeter of the clearing. She found a faint game trail heading down one of the steep slopes opposite the trailhead. She thanked Tee. He was always exploring game trails, trying to figure out what their purpose was. This one meant there was a hidden way off the cliff.

If she was lucky, it would lead to water, which might then lead downstream toward Apple Lake. It might not be easy, but it was a better plan than waiting for the GEMs. Hopefully, the game trail didn't circle back to the cliff trail. Crossing her fingers, she carefully eased her way down the steep trail. She was careful not to fall or disturb anything that might be used to track her.

With luck, the GEMs wouldn't be as good at wood craft as she was.

The game trail led to a small stream and then alongside it downhill. It was narrow but eventually widened out enough that Diana could jog if she kept the pace slow and was careful. It suddenly veered south and past a small waterfall. She recognized the waterfall and headed off toward where the main trail should be. The main trail appeared suddenly and with that, she was running as fast as she could toward Apple Lake.

CHAPTER 21

INVASION

Griff was observing Scout Team 2 performing climbing and repelling exercises. The team was working their way up the steep cliffs near the eastern sea. It wasn't far from Apple Falls. This area was perfect for this type of training because the granite walls were sheer, with just enough imperfections in them to allow for pitons to be driven in for support, but not enough to make a path to the top easy. You had to select your path carefully. It was grueling exercise.

The entire team knew they were there because of the bar brawl. Over the past month, just when they thought their punishment was over, Griff would show up and take them on another exhausting venture. He called it training. They knew it was punishment.

Griff was pleased with Sergeant Glenn's handling of all this. He had punished the offending members appropriately and never complained about Griff's extra assignments. Griff was delighted by the brawl, although he would never admit it. In his opinion, Jay and Kale were the future of non-com leadership.

The two of them thrashing five seasoned veterans from one of the better scout teams sent a strong message. Even better was that the brawl started because of insults thrown at Tee. News of this would make Tee's entry into the officer ranks easier. He ordered them all to be silent. But he knew that just meant they would whisper about it instead of talking openly.

Just then, he noticed smoke on the horizon above the cliff edge. It was in the general direction of where a signal fire might be, so he ordered Scout Team 2 to repel back down immediately. When down, they took off at a run for Apple Falls. The team of fourteen scouts plus himself rode the Tram up the lower falls. This thing is useful, thought Griff, silently thanking Del. Once on the road, they ran to Apple Valley, which was in total chaos when they arrived.

Major Richards and Arti were trying to organize, but the crowd was out of control. Griff's booming voice called out, "QUIET!" One of the burly villagers turned in his direction and kept shouting, so Griff walked up and coldcocked him. Casually placing his boot on the unconscious man's chest, he asked with malice in his voice, "Anyone else have an opinion?" That shut everyone up.

"Major Richards, what is the situation?" Griff demanded.

"A couple of hunters surprised GEM scouts up by the upper southeast beach lookout. One of them ran to the southernmost cliff lookout and, not finding anyone, lit the signal fire. She saw three large troop transport ships heading for the southeast beach. We were just discussing whether to attack their position or set up a defense."

"We don't have time for a debate. If they get control of the upper east valley we're screwed," Griff said with disgust. Griff then barked out orders to Richards, "Select fifty warriors and ten archers based on their endurance. I will take this advance team to the beach lookout and engage. Send another fifty warriors and ten archers at a quick march behind the advance team as a reserve. Assign a leader for the reserve team. All others are going to set up a defensive line blocking the upper east valley entry into the main valley just above the falls. Richards, you are in charge of the defense. Arti, stay here and support Richards. Assign leaders to be in charge of the archers for the advance and reserve attack teams."

Everyone started moving at once. Although Richards was officially in charge, nobody questioned Griff's orders, including Richards. In minutes, Griff and the advance team were jogging up the trail to the upper east valley. He had wanted to have Arti with the Reserve team. But he had lost all confidence in Richards. He thought she would keep things under control now that they had a plan. He shook his head. Richards had to go.

Puffing heavily as he ran up the trail, Griff had to admit he was impressed. The majority of the Advance Team was keeping up with Scout Team 2. The leader of the Advance Team Archers was a young woman named Diana. He remembered her from when he had delivered the recruiting invite to Tee.

At first, he thought she was too young for this assignment. But it turned out she was one of the hunters who surprised the GEM scouts. That she and her hunting partner had killed three of them was impressive. It had been her idea to split up with her partner, warning Apple Valley while she went to light the signal fire. Since she had no idea if that outpost had also been overrun, it was incredibly brave.

So far, they had been lucky. Devine intervention level of luck. He realized a full-scale invasion of the upper peninsula was detected because Diana's boyfriend was a lousy hunter, and she had superb judgement and courage. He prayed for their 'luck' to continue.

Diana had been a good choice for leader of the Advance Team Archers, thought Griff. As an avid hunter, she knew the area extremely well. She correctly guessed where the GEMs might place pickets. Which allowed them to be quickly taken out without setting off alarms. Better yet, she knew a back way into the beach lookout they could use to their advantage. Griff sent Staff Sergeant Glenn with six other scouts, five of the archers including Diana, and ten volunteers, all known to be good hunters. They would know how to sneak up on the beach cliff top without making noise.

"Stay hidden until you see them pursue our retreat," Griff told the team tasked with sneaking around the back. Your objective is to cut the rope ladders that will likely be in place. While we want to kick them all off the cliff as quickly as possible, it's more important to slow their progress up the cliff."

Turning to the main group, he said, "Main attack group will engage and then fall back into a defensive position. The main attack team archers will stay at the defensive position and cover the retreat. Your job is to slow the GEMs down as much as you can so the men can take their positions. Our goal is to draw the bulk of them away from the cliff. It's critical for us to buy time for our reinforcements to arrive."

Sergeant Glenn motioned Diana to his side as they carefully made their way up the back entrance trail. He whispered in her ear, "Follow us to the trail opening after the attack begins. Group your women on both sides of the trail as it opens up on the clearing on the summit. We will already be engaged when you get visuals on the GEMs, but provide whatever support you can. Your main role is to help cover our retreat."

Diana considered this for a moment and said, "I know the area. With a little time, I can have our archers dispersed along the entire back side of the clearing. We can hide far enough back in the foliage to blend in, but still have clear lines of sight. If we open the attack with a flight of arrows, they will be confused and looking for cover. If we are properly positioned, they won't be able to tell where the arrows are coming from. That should soften them up a bit for your attack."

Sergeant Glenn's thinking was much like most members of the Guard. Wall Archers had their place. Their place was up on the Wall, doing what they could in a support role. It wasn't generating battle plans. It wasn't leadership. But her plan sounded like an improvement. If the archers were discovered while dispersing, they could immediately launch the sudden assault he was envisioning, with little downside. Diana's plan had a chance of creating confusion and, with luck, panic.

Hesitating for a few moments to think it through, he said quietly, "I like it. Let me get into position before you disperse your archers. If you are detected, we'll attack immediately. Do you have some way of coordinating the first flight of arrows?"

"Yes. I can use a signaling arrow. It creates a high-pitched whistle. I'll launch that at your signal, and the other archers will launch immediately. I've told them to look to you for direction once we're engaged. If you want us to concentrate on any specific target or area, just wave and point. If not, they will pick off random targets as quickly as they can in support of you cutting the rope ladders," Diana whispered.

As soon as Sergeant Glenn gave her the hand signal Diana let her signaling arrow fly. She hit what she guessed was the senior GEM square in the back, driving him to his knees. Arrows sprouted immediately on GEMs located near the ropes anchored on the cliff edge. Her team was operating in what Arti called zones. Each woman took out everything in her zone until it was empty. They then moved to the right or left adjacent zones based on volume of targets. Sergeant Glenn had decided to use the whistling arrow to launch the ground attack as well. By the time Glenn and his attack team got to the cliff edge, most of the GEMs left behind were down or wounded.

There was a brief, brutal skirmish to take out those GEMs left who could still fight. The ropes were quickly cut, which elicited loud screams from below the cliff edge. Glenn immediately called for a retreat, and they hurried back toward the narrow trail they had used to sneak up the back side of the cliff. The archers quickly abandoned their posts and took their own paths back to the trail, weaving their way through the trees and stones. Sergeant Glenn had initially argued that they should stay and make the GEMs fight two separate battle lines. Griff had countermanded that saying Glenn's objective was to cut the ropes with as few losses as possible and then rejoin the main group. "Once the ropes are cut, they won't be able to replace them before our reserves arrive."

Griff was pleased. Unlike most plans, this one had been executed more or less as designed. The initial attack had drawn thirty or so GEMs away from the cliff edge and the rope ladders had been successfully cut. The change he made on the fly was to abandon his defensive position and throw everything into an all-out attack.

Once the rope ladders had been cut, screams from the falling GEMs had alerted them that they had been flanked. This had drawn the bulk of the GEMs back toward the cliff. Now that he had an idea how many GEMs were there, he confidently took the initiative. He was delighted to see Glenn had called off his own retreat once he realized Griff was attacking. Caught between the two battle lines, the GEMs had been quickly and efficiently dispatched. He noticed that many of the GEMs near the cliff edge had arrows in them.

When he first looked down over the cliff, he saw hundreds of GEMs on the beach. The sight made him shiver. From the bodies at the base of the cliff, quite a few had been on the rope ladders when they were cut. The trebuchet intended to harass ships attempting to land on the beach had been destroyed by the GEMs. But they hadn't bothered with the piles of stones stored for that purpose.

Glenn had the volunteers throwing these down into the crowd of GEMs milling around in confusion below. He also had a group gathering the dead GEMs up and chucking them over the cliff as well. A brutal message and an efficient way to clean up the mess. The ocean would do the work of disposing of GEM bodies for them. Knowing they had lost their chance, the GEMs organized themselves, turned around, and were going back to their ships for a retreat to sea.

"Sergeant Glenn, casualties report," Griff said firmly.

"One volunteer from my team killed and eight from the main attack team. Another ten wounded. Guard scouts are okay with Bill having a minor wound he's already taken care of. None of the volunteer wounds are life threatening, although two may need a doctor's attention before we try and move them back to Apple Valley," Glenn reported.

"The archers?" Griff asked.

"None killed or wounded. Diana spread the advance team out along the back of the clearing and far enough back in the woods that the GEMs couldn't tell where the arrows were coming from. She was perched on an outcropping so she could see the entire clearing. The rest were hiding behind bushes, rocks, and tree trunks. They made taking out the GEMs left behind after the initial assault easy. We just had to finish a few off and cut the ropes. Those women are deadly!" Glenn said with a smile, admiration shining in his eyes.

As the sergeant was finishing his report, Diana wandered over and showed them two dozen special arrows the women had brought. "Should we try and set those ships on fire?" she asked. The arrows had blown glass vial arrow heads filled with a flammable liquid. Oil-soaked rags were wound tightly around the shaft just below the arrow heads.

"Let them fly," Griff said with a determined grin. "But pick one of the ships and focus on starting fires that are spread out. You'll need to create enough separate fires to overwhelm their ability to fight the flames."

Two of the ships got away, but the third caught fire and was eventually taken by the sea with all hands. The other two ships didn't even attempt to save anyone. Griff wondered again if a full-time archers auxiliary ought to be part of the Guard. It was silliness not to include them in scout teams. Their value in situations like this was enormous. Most of the Guard belittled the women's abilities and contributions. Well, Glenn was certainly a convert. Griff took a deep breath and told himself it was another quest to be put on the back burner for now.

Griff didn't let them cut down the four lookout guards until the reserve team showed up. He wanted everyone to see what happens when you aren't diligent. More than a few people had to step into the forest to empty their stomachs. Evidently, the southern cliff lookout had been abandoned for a card game. From the mess in the guard shack, the four had been drinking and playing cards when they were surprised. The attack was likely a small boat floating in at night, then pulled up high on the beach out of sight.

A few of the GEMs must have climbed the challenging cliff at night and surprised the lookouts. Four horribly mutilated bodies were tied to trees just outside the shack. The GEMs had taken their time. It was obvious the four lookouts died horribly. They all heard the stories of what GEMs did to prisoners. But seeing it firsthand was gruesome. Griff ordered the four to be cremated in the signal fire pit.

They didn't deserve a resting place in the Hall of Heroes, and he didn't want their families to see how they had died. It seemed appropriate that their final resting place would put them on lookout duty for eternity.

I deserve to be in that fire pit as well, thought Griff. One derelict lookout team was bad. But two at the same time was hard to accept. Richards was clearly not keeping up with his duties. But this was incompetence that went beyond one person. When he was here the last time, he should have spent a week hiking to all the lookout spots and performing surprise inspections. He suspected things might be a little lax, and he had a responsibility to chase that suspicion down.

Griff shook off his guilt. It wasn't the time for self-recrimination. He could beat himself up later. A major probe like this was highly unusual, and he wondered if it was part of some larger objective. It was time to anticipate the worst and mobilize at the Wall.

"Sergeant, I need to get to Landfall City as soon as possible. Get both lookouts cleaned up and provisioned. Scour this area and make sure we don't have any GEMs hiding in the woods. Diana can recommend volunteers who know this area your team can work with. You are in charge until orders from the Guard arrive. You understand?"

"Yes, Master Sergeant," Glenn said, then hesitating he offered, "I'll tell Major Richards I'm operating on your orders until I hear from the Guard."

Griff nodded and said, "I'll likely see you at the Wall. Good luck." Griff turned away and headed down the trail toward Apple Valley. The fact that Glenn understood his intent immediately was proof Richards's ineffectiveness was obvious to everyone. He really should have done something sooner.

CHAPTER 22

COUNCIL VOTE

Del was surprised when Griff walked into his office. The master sergeant was a meticulous man. He was always clean shaven with a perfectly pressed uniform. He looked like he had slept in this one. Maybe rolled around in the dirt a bit, too. He looked worn out and sleep deprived. The smell of horse sweat now permeated his office. Del would usually start off with banter. The state of the uniform, the three-day-old beard, or the smell would be good places to start. However, something was seriously wrong here.

"What's wrong, Griff?" Del said with concern in his eyes.

"We need to mobilize, but I can't get CGG's support to go to the president to propose it," Griff said abruptly.

"Back up. Why do we need to mobilize?" Del asked.

"Three days ago, we fought off an attack in Apple Valley at the southernmost upper east side beach lookout. There were five to six hundred GEMs on the beach when we finally threw their advance team off the cliff. I believe this is part of something bigger," Griff said.

Del was shocked. Three days to get from Apple Valley to the capital meant he had been on horseback without sleep since he left. Griff wasn't prone to overreaction, so Del cautioned himself to listen carefully.

"What makes you think this is something major?" Del

prompted.

"There were three ships involved in the landfall. Two of them sported a common flag, but the third was different. That means at least two war lords are cooperating. As you know, this is unheard of. Next, their target is strange. Strategically gaining control of one of the upper east valleys is limiting. While highly defendable, the valley is also a bottleneck if you're trying to get out. In other words, it's an excellent fort but almost as good of a jail."

"Why would they want to do that?" Del asked.

"It potentially pulls warriors away from the Wall. They are smart and have been watching us for as long as we've been watching them. They know if they capture even a small inconsequential piece of land, we'll throw everything against them until we kick them out. As you know, it would take six days, best case, to call troops back from Apple Lake. It's a clever diversion. My guess is that they will accelerate a major assault against the Wall once they hear of their failure to take the upper east valley. I believe we have less than a week to start mobilizing."

"We have watchers up on Mount Anderson with an antique telescope looking for GEM movement," Del said. "So far, we haven't seen any signs. In fact, it's been unusually quiet."

"That's just another sign of trouble, Del. Why should it be quiet? They know they have attacked us up north. They are obviously trying to lull us into a false sense of security at the Wall," Griff said.

As Griff started to add to his explanation, Del held up his hand to pause the conversation. He needed to think. How much could he tell Griff? He suspected Griff was right based on developments he had become aware of just that morning. But he couldn't reveal his knowledge of events beyond the limits of the telescope up on Mount Anderson. Griff's analysis was solid. Del was impressed once again with Griff's intelligence. Unfortunately, his arguments were weak in terms of what was politically acceptable. Mobilizations were very expensive and extraordinarily disruptive. The early spring planting season would start in a few weeks and none of the agricultural districts would be happy with a disruption. The council would want hard evidence of an impending attack before committing to a full-scale mobilization.

Del eventually looked up with determination. "I'll go see the president. It's better if I go alone because she is new and a bit suspicious of the military," Del said, the lie coming easily. "Give me a full rundown of the attack and walk me through your logic one more time."

After carefully describing the events surrounding the upper east valley, Griff added, "Since I'm in charge of training, it's within my authority to call a special Guard training event at the Wall. The CGG will be pissed off. Probably turn purple yelling at me. But he won't countermand it because he specifically gave me that authority. At least the Guard can be mobilized."

Del walked briskly from his office in the university to the small unassuming building that housed Pacifica's Administration, Judiciary, and Council functions. The military was a separate function reporting into administration. The president led government administration. Each of these functions was strictly limited by Pacifica's constitution. The original colonizers were minimalists when it came to government.

The constitution conferred specific authorities to each function and clearly stated that any powers not specifically conferred did not exist. They adhered in spirit to Plato's belief that governments are best led by philosophers. The idea being that government was a civic duty that should be completely separate from personal power and monetary considerations. Therefore, all civil servants took a vow of dependance on government support for their lifetime. They discarded all personal wealth, current or future.

The original colonists from Ships 1 and 3 had studied the long history of governmental failure and agreed that money was indeed the root of all evil. Therefore, public servants had political power but could not benefit financially from it. Since the constitution had a balanced budget requirement, this meant the size of government was forced to be small, frugal, and efficient.

Del walked into the president's office and asked the receptionist for the soonest appointment available. Turned out she had an opening in thirty minutes, so Del just sat down and waited.

Jennifer Malrey walked out of her office and greeted Del warmly. She was young and newly elected to her role. Although small in stature, she tended to fill the room with her presence without being intimidating. It was a calm and comforting presence.

The President of Pacifica was a ten-year term with no term limits. It typically only ended with death, retirement, or a vote of no confidence by the Pacifica Council. The previous president had retired after thirty years and was now serving Jennifer in a support role. This was common in Pacifica. Becoming a civil servant was a lifetime decision.

"It's good to see you, Professor. Come on in," President Malrey said, motioning him into her office. After they sat down at a table, she said, "What can I help you with?"

"It's not good news. I strongly believe we need to call for full mobilization," Del said with gravity.

"I haven't heard of any sightings," she said, confused.

"There was an attack we fought off in the Apple Valley region. They attacked one of the few beach sites and succeeded in reaching the top of the cliffs. Fortunately, they were defeated and retreated back to the sea. There is more to the story, but I strongly recommend calling the council together for a decision," Del said.

The president thought about this for a few moments and said, "We're lucky. All of the council members are currently in the capital. In another week, they would all have been home on spring recess. I'll call an emergency meeting. Can you come to the council chambers this evening after their regular sessions end?"

"Yes. I'll also go down to Guard headquarters and bring the CGG back with me. His opinion and advice might be needed," Del said.

"Thanks for bringing this to my attention. I sincerely hope we don't need to mobilize. But if there is evidence of a threat, we need to act," she said.

"One last item, Ms. President," Del said in a hushed voice, "The committee has just gotten evidence this morning strongly supporting the need to mobilize. As you know, I won't be presenting that evidence to the council members."

She rocked back slightly, locked eyes with him, and then said a voice that didn't go any further than Del's ears, "Understood."

There was a regular Tram that went between Landfall City and Guard headquarters down by the Wall. It was water powered and similar to the one traversing Apple

Falls. The difference is that this one was larger, simpler, and faster, given the elevation change wasn't as extreme. This cut travel time down to a couple of hours, enough time to fetch the CGG and bring him back for the council meeting. Del would have to tread carefully. The CGG was a reasonable man, but one under the shadow of Griff, which irritated him. He would have to explain this as his concern rather than Griff's while using the information from the raid to support the need for mobilization. Everyone told him he was good at politics. It was not something he enjoyed.

Perhaps that is why he liked Griff as much as he did. No BS, just say what you think and work it out from there. Of course, Griff had his own agenda, just like everyone else. The difference was that Griff didn't hide his. All of his agendas were out in the open for everyone to see.

Del noticed that the council members were tired. They were at the end of a long day and nearing a much-needed recess. He couldn't decide if this was a good thing or not. It might make them more disagreeable, or it might make them open to good arguments. He would just have to wait and see how it played out.

There were a total of six council members, two from each region. When they formed the first government, a debate had sprung up on how to make sure their government didn't end up controlled by a patriarchy. While the original colonists thought of themselves as non-biased and open-minded, history was riddled with male dominated governments. It was pointed out that a healthy family consists of equal partners, each having their own responsibilities. So, the proposal was to have each region elect one man and one woman as representatives. Men would vote for the male representative and women would vote for the female. All other democratically elected positions, like president, were open to all. Just the main council was forced by the constitution to be split equally by sex. To the surprise of many, this worked amazingly well.

President Malrey walked in, sat down at the head of the council table, and brought it to order. "Thank you for staying late after a long day. The agenda tonight is an emergency proposal for full mobilization at the Wall. We have two guests. Professor Dacy brought this request and will review why he believes full mobilization is required. Our Commander General of the Guard is here to answer any questions on mobilization timing and alternatives."

Councilman Barlow, one of the representatives from Eureka, raised his hand and said, "Ms. President, might I request that we expand this discussion to include plans to negotiate for peace with the GEMs?"

"I am happy to table that discussion for another time, Councilman Barlow. Our work tonight is time critical. We need to quickly come to a decision on mobilization," President Malrey replied.

"I propose a vote to overrule your decision to limit the agenda to mobilization. The proposal is to include plans to negotiate with the GEMs," Councilman Barlow said in a challenging tone.

The president's role within the council was to organize, facilitate, and vote to break ties. She owned presenting and keeping the council on track with a clear and concise agenda. The council could overrule and propose an alternative agenda if four of the six councilpersons agreed. The president would then facilitate the new agenda to completion. Any of the six councilpersons could propose an alternative agenda.

"Okay, let's vote on whether to include discussions and possible votes on a GEM negotiation strategy, or offer," President Malrey said. They then went around the table with each councilperson voting on the altered agenda.

"Apple Councilwoman Ricks?"

"Nay. We were informed of an invasion of one of the Apple Lakes upper valleys by the Master Sergeant of the Guard. It's clear we need to be worried about our survival, not ridiculous proposals for peace," Ricks responded with anger in her voice.

"Apple Councilman Rickets?"

"Nay. Agree with Councilwoman Ricks. Let's get on with the proposed agenda."

"Eureka Councilwoman Rivers?"

"Nay. But I agree with Councilman Barlow that we need to consider concessions for peace. I would like to see a future agenda on this topic."

"Eureka Councilman Barlow?"

"Yea. We must stop acting like children and find a way to end these brutal wars."

"Landfall Councilwoman Pierce?"

"Nay. Our survival comes before any fantasies of peace with the GEMs."

"Landfall Councilman Barrett?"

"Nay. Peace negotiations are worth time on another day. I see little evidence they would be successful, but that doesn't mean we shouldn't try."

"The Nays carry the vote. Professor Dacy, you have the floor."

Del described the assault on the upper east valley in

detail. He made sure to vividly describe the mutilation of the four lookouts. Then he mentioned the evidence of war lords cooperating in the assault. This caused a few gasps. One of Pacifica's perceived advantages was the historic inability of the GEMs to cooperate across the various tribes. That advantage was now in question.

Councilman Barlow raised his hand and, turning to the CGG, asked, "Was your master sergeant in charge of the assault on the GEMs?"

"Yes. We were extremely fortunate that he was training a scout team close by. If not, we would likely have an entire valley full of GEMs to worry about now," the CGG said.

"Did he try to negotiate with the GEMs before slaughtering them?" Barlow asked with anger clearly evident.

"We don't negotiate with GEMs. We kill them," the CGG fired back.

"Well, perhaps that's the problem."

As Barlow opened his mouth to say more, President Malrey raised her hand, interrupting him. Then she firmly said, "Councilman Barlow. Please control yourself and stay on the agenda. We voted to table discussions of peace negotiations for another time."

He mumbled something, clearly very angry, but complied with her request. Del then presented a completely fabricated analysis showing a high probability of an immediate and large-scale assault on the Wall.

Del ended with a summary. "Observations from Mount Anderson show haze consistent with a large encampment just over the horizon. While there might be a natural meteorological reason for this, it would be unusual at this time of year. Our long-term analysis suggests that with their reproduction rates and expected mortality, the GEMs are likely running out of room. Instead of just coveting the peninsula, it is highly likely they need the space and agricultural output to support their growing population. My belief is that extreme conditions inland are forcing the war lords to cooperate. This will greatly enhance their ability to break through at the Wall."

"Are there any questions for Professor Dacy or the CGG?" President Malrey asked.

Councilwoman Rivers raised her hand and, when recognized, asked, "Can we discuss alternatives for a limited mobilization? It's close to the start of planting season. A full mobilization will mean our food stores could be diminished for up to eighteen months."

Jennifer nodded. "That is a reasonable request. However, let's vote on the proposal for a full mobilization and then table other alternatives, as necessary."

It was a split vote. As Del feared, the agricultural concerns of Landfall and Eureka overwhelmed their fear of a major assault on the Wall. He knew this was predicated on confidence that the Guard could hold off the GEMs long enough for a full mobilization if needed. Del had not worked with Jennifer for very long. He didn't know what she would do. The right move politically would be to abstain and table more palatable alternatives.

An expectation of the president is that they do everything possible so that a final decision was a majority vote by the council. Something that was jointly hashed out. Del was sure some level of mobilization would pass. This is what the council expected. While not everyone would be happy, they would all be satisfied.

President Malrey took a deep breath. She looked down at the table in front of her for a few moments, obviously collecting her thoughts. "We are deadlocked, but I am convinced the threat is real. I vote Yea."

Del could see that a few of the council members felt betrayed. This went against the long-standing practice of ending with a majority vote. There was a general belief that deadlocked proposals merely meant further negotiation and compromise was needed. It was rare for a president to be the final deciding vote on a major topic. She had to be careful because the council could force an election off cycle with a vote of no confidence. This only took a majority vote and was a real threat.

As they walked out of the council chambers, Del turned to the CGG and said quietly, "Well, we have a gutsy president."

"Thank God! I think we're going to need one," said the CGG. "You obviously think Griff is right about the upper east valley attack being part of a larger strategy."

"Yes, I do. We have tracked major assaults on the Wall over the years. Its past due for one and the size of the army attacking us has grown larger with every cycle," Del said.

"My biggest worry now is that they won't show up. That would create an atmosphere of suspicion of anything the Guard or university proposes in the future," the CGG said.

"I'm not hoping they show up. But I don't want our recommendations to be ignored in the future either. It's a lose-lose scenario," Del said. "We'll just have to focus on mobilizing. I truly hope we're lucky enough to end up with loud and divisive arguments instead of the alternative."

CHAPTER 23

MOBILIZATION

Apple Valley was in an uproar. There had been many partial mobilizations over the years. But this was the first major one in twelve years. Arti was spending as much time calming people down as she was planning the trip to the Wall. Thank goodness for Diana, she thought. That girl was a godsend. Arti had known Diana would eventually replace her as Apple Valley CA, Captain of Archers. But in the midst of the chaos, Arti realized how good that decision was.

Diana had organized the packing of their extensive store of bows, arrows, and support equipment. In addition to their existing supplies, they had to bring along all the tools and raw materials to make the wide variety of arrows that might be needed. This involved gathering all the women together and assigning them tasks. She showed real leadership. It allowed Arti to work with Major Richards and get everyone else organized for the long trip to the Wall. Major Richards was still in charge but had delegated much of his responsibilities to Arti, which was a good thing for the Apple Valley Volunteers.

"Diana, is everything ready to go?" Arti asked.

"Yes. We're first up for the Tram tomorrow morning. I'll have all the packing cases down there by nightfall," Diana replied, wiping sweat from her brow. "Most of the unit has already started down the trail and when the supplies show up in the morning, we won't waste any time getting started."

"Did Tia's parents agree with her joining us?" Diana asked in a hopeful voice. Full mobilization meant they would bring the arrow monkeys with them. These were girls who had shown interest and aptitude in becoming Wall Archers. They repaired equipment, made arrows, and supplied everything needed to the archers on the Wall.

"Tia has been harassing them non-stop since the call for mobilization came out," Arti said with a smile. "I was her age when I first went to the Wall as an arrow monkey. My brother clearly remembers it and feels it's time for her to get the experience."

Arti hesitated and then said, "Pete is the only one unhappy. He's going to work behind the Wall supplying food and water in the mess hall. He'll also train with the boys' reserve unit on his downtime. They never see any time on the Wall, but it's good training. You know Pete, he was going on and on about being good enough to fight on the Wall. I think he's jealous of Tia being able to work on the Wall at such a young age," Arti said.

"He'll get over it. Pete wants to do his part. He imagines his part should be bigger than it is. He'll be an excellent warrior someday, but he's still a boy," Diana said, smiling. Then, in a serious tone, "Ansen is a bit unsettled. Angry. Facing those GEMs made it all very real for both of us. My nightmares were pretty bad for a while. It was the same one every night. I'm being chased through the woods by GEMs and suddenly realize they have me trapped. I'm not going to get away. Then I wake up in a panic. One night in my dream, I turned and fought. I haven't had that nightmare since."

She hesitated a few moments and then said, "I wonder if Ansen is dealing with something like that. He changes the subject every time I bring that day up."

"Men can be hard to figure out. They appear to be strong and tough, a rock to stand beside in hard times. But at the same time, they can hide their fear. It can slowly tear them apart," Arti said softly. "Anger comes from fear. Keep trying to get him to talk about it. I'll talk to Grammy and encourage her to sit down with him before he heads off."

"Grammy really helped me with all of it. She has a way of putting things into perspective," Diana said, then changing topics she asked, "Will we run into trouble in Eureka Valley?"

"Had a long talk with Councilwoman Ricks about the troubles down there. She said Councilman Barlow has been stirring up the farmers. He's telling them they are going to suffer two years of hardship as a result of Apple Valley overreacting. Barlow claims we convinced the university to conspire with the Guard to overstate the risk," Arti said with frustration. "He says Del's an Apple Valley bigot and is using the university's prestige to force the mobilization. He's saying President Malrey is young and naïve. She's been fooled by the university. He questions her ability to lead.

"That's unfair," Diana said. "I don't think the university, or the Guard, would create a problem that doesn't exist."

"I agree. The protests have been peaceful so far. She thinks portions of Eureka will defy the council and only do a partial mobilization. Hold enough of their volunteers back to ensure a good harvest next fall. Ricks plans to ask the council to censure Barlow if that happens. In the meantime, our plan is to travel in small groups. That's why we're traveling separately from the men's volunteer corp. We'll camp away from the cities on our way down. Once we get to Landfall Valley, it will be calmer."

"There was a rumor that Ricks was going to pick her bow back up," Diana said, grinning.

"She actually asked me if she could rejoin for the battle," Arti said, smiling back. "I laughed and asked her if she had been practicing. She admitted it had been a while since she picked up her bow. I gave her my stern instructor look and offered to let her try the Wall Archers qualification test. She held up her hands in mock horror and told me she had barely passed the test fifty years ago. She laughed and offered that maybe it was best if she just made sure the council gives us what we need."

"She's older than Grammy but I can see her on the Wall with a bow," Diana said smiling, "That is one tough woman."

"That she is. We couldn't have a better councilwoman," Arti said with admiration.

Arti was pleased with the speed and ease of travel through Eureka Valley until they got to Leucadia. To avoid the town, they would have had to add a day to their travel time and were under orders to get to the Wall as soon as possible. Until the GEMs actually showed up, they would hurry but not exhaust themselves. The plan was to camp an hour north of the city and traverse it in the early hours before the sun came up.

The hope of avoiding conflict ended early the next morning when a large contingent of Eureka Valley farmers blocked the road just outside the town's entrance. "I guess getting up early in the morning isn't the best way to avoid farmers," Arti said with a wry expression on her face.

"What are we going to do?" Diana asked.

Arti turned to her and said, "What would you recommend?"

It's mentoring time again, thought Diana wryly. She stopped and gave it some thought. After reflecting on the alternatives, she said, "I would stop, set up camp, and force them to make the next move. If they don't approach us, we'll just wait until the next company of Apple Valley volunteers shows up and decide whether to force the issue or not," Diana said thoughtfully.

"You're on the right trail, Diana. The only thing I would change is to go ask them for permission to use the road and see what happens. We'll ask respectfully, listen, but not argue." Arti paused a moment and then added, "But first, let's make it clear we're setting up camp so that any hotheads over there don't have an excuse to escalate the situation. They are unlikely to attack women, but you never know what angry people will do. Meet me here in an hour and we'll go talk to them."

Arti and Diana walked slowly up to a large cart set sideways on the road. There were about thirty men sitting around a fire off to one side, watching them as they approached. One of the older ones got to his feet and, with an entourage of younger men, approached them well in front of the cart.

"Do you need some help getting your broken cart off the road?" Arti said with a smile.

"This isn't the time for jokes, Arti. Yes, I recognize you, Arti Stone. Turn around and go back to Apple Valley. We have no beef with the Wall Archers. You Apple Valley people are overreacting to a few GEMs climbing a cliff. Full mobilization now will cause many of us in the Eureka Valley to go hungry next winter. Fruit trees will continue to produce crops regardless of whether you take a spring vacation to the Wall."

"Since you know my name, can I have yours?" Arti asked in a calm voice.

"My name is Will Evans and I'm mayor of Leucadia."

"We're not arguing for you to join us," Arti pointed out.

"No, but a message needs to be sent to the president and her council. We aren't going to stand for an unnecessary full mobilization that unfairly punishes us and our families," Will said angrily. "Councilman Barlow has explained how you used the university dean and the Guard to scare the government into mobilizing."

"Okay, I understand your position, Will. We're going to camp here and wait for the council to resolve your issues. We don't want conflict. We aren't responsible for the mobilization. But we are obligated to support the council's decision," Arti said.

Will visibly relaxed, realizing Arti wasn't going to press the issue. "I have a lot of respect for you and your Wall Archers, Arti. This isn't personal," Will said in a placating voice. "If you need supplies from town, we'll let a few people through for that."

"I appreciate your flexibility and thoughtfulness, Will. Apple Valley wouldn't survive without its trade with Eureka Valley. We greatly appreciate all that you do," Arti said, smiling back at him.

Will brightened and actually smiled at the compliment, waving goodbye as they turned and walked away. As Diana and Arti headed back to camp, Diana turned to Arti. "Well, you charmed him. He went from belligerent to flirting," she said, with the corners of her mouth turning up.

"Men are men, Diana. Let them blow off steam, acknowledge their point of view, and then compliment them. It works every time. Another of Grammy's lessons," Arti said with a smirk. They both chuckled as they entered the camp.

The next morning Arti wandered down to the road blockade, intending to try to work out some sort of compromise when she saw a commotion in town. She squinted her eyes, trying to see what was going on, and then smiled. It was Griff with Scout Team 2 on horseback, moving quickly toward the blocked road from the other side. She recognized the scout team from the upper east valley invasion. Griff looked especially grumpy.

Griff skidded to a stop just behind the cart, recognized and nodded to Arti, turned and demanded in a commanding voice, "Whose cart is this?"

The crowd of farmers looked around at each other for a few uncomfortable moments. Will Evans grunted and turned toward Griff. "Doesn't matter whose cart it is. It's not moving."

Griff got off his horse and walked slowly, but with a belligerent swagger up to Will. Arti was impressed with how threatening Griff could be without saying a word. It was especially appealing knowing his secret. Griff was actually a softy. He stopped and stared at the man for a moment and then said, "Who are you?"

"My name is Will Evans and I'm the mayor of Leucadia," he said in an angry voice.

"Who is the assistant mayor?" Griff said.

"Why do you want to know?" Will answered with his chin thrust forward but a bit of reluctance in his stance.

"Because after I execute you for interfering with a

mandated mobilization, I need to know who to talk to next," Griff said, stepping closer, daring the man to do something.

Both of Will's hands shot up palms forward as he took a step back and spluttered out, "You can't just kill me. We have a right to protest."

"You do have the right to protest. You don't have the right to obstruct a council ordered mobilization. The law is clear. If a citizen interferes with Pacifica's ability to wage war, including mobilization efforts, summary execution is an option at the discretion of the highest-ranking Guard member present," Griff said as he pulled out his sword. "As Master Sergeant of the Guard, I have the authority to act."

Will put up both hands, backing away quickly. "Okay, we'll move the cart and leave."

"You and your followers will not leave," Griff said, sweeping his gaze around to lock eyes with all of them. You are ordered to the Wall to protect Pacifica." Griff then looked over his shoulder and barked out, "Sergeant Glenn! Round up these volunteers. Take each of them home to get their weapons and provisions. Make sure none of them sneak off. If any of them try to avoid their obligations, bring them to me for judgement." Turning back to the mayor, Griff said, "I'm confiscating the cart for your equipment and provisions. You need to supply a couple of horses to pull it."

Will was defeated and speechless. When Griff took a step toward him, he quickly turned and motioned to a couple of the young men to pull the cart off the road. Arti glanced over at Sergeant Glenn and his team. She saw amusement dancing on their faces. I bet they have all been on the other side of Griff's displeasure, thought Arti.

After the logistics had been worked out, Arti walked back to camp with Griff. "You aren't the most subtle of men," Arti said with a serious expression on her face.

"There are times when the direct approach works best," he replied uncertainly. Griff was obviously unclear whether Arti was displeased with his actions or not.

Arti couldn't hold it, and her face broke into a smile and said, "I imagine the direct approach works really well for you in most circumstances." Then, hesitating a moment, she said softly, "Thank you Griff. We were stuck. You did exactly what was needed. We have to get to the Wall, not get embroiled in a political discussion." Griff blushed and Arti moved closer as they walked toward the Wall Archer camp together. Arti turned toward Griff and asked in a soft voice. "How is Tee?"

"Healthy and working hard," Griff replied, then remembering the bar brawl, smiled and said, "Don't tell him I told you this, but he's developing into a good leader. The veterans are noticing how much the Newbies in his class respect him and that bodes well for his acceptance."

Arti smiled with pride. Her husband had died before they had more children, and that pained her. But she was blessed with her only son. Satisfied Tee was doing well, her mind transitioned back to Griff walking beside her. He was all work and no play. Being honest with herself, this was an observation that accurately described her as well. Now that Tee was an adult on his own, perhaps it was time to live a little.

She was very attracted to Griff. She knew he was kindhearted when she first met him. Not sure how she knew this, given his fearsome reputation, but she knew. He was intelligent, thoughtful, and his insights on a wide range of topics were interesting. It didn't hurt that he was a ruggedly handsome man who took great care of his appearance. She had always liked the rugged look, and cleanliness was a big deal to her. When he was close, she ran the risk of turning back into the giddy teenager she had once been. She knew Griff had never been married and wondered about that. Lifelong bachelors were more common in the Guard. It was a hard life that made it difficult to have a family.

For a man with such a brutal exterior, he seemed to be exceedingly shy around women. She was pretty sure he liked women, and she in particular. The occasional flush of his face, hard to see with his dark skin, betrayed him. Well, perhaps after this upcoming battle with the GEMs is over, she would have to make a move. The worst thing that could happen was embarrassment, after all.

The rest of their travel down to the Wall was uneventful. Griff and Scout Team 2 decided to travel with them. They rode out early each morning and returned as camp was being set up in the evening. Traffic on the road was increasing substantially. It was pretty obvious that whatever Griff and Scout Team 2 were doing was accelerating Eureka Valley mobilization.

Diana and Sergeant Glenn had taken to sitting by one of the campfires most nights and talking. "Where do you go every day?" Diana asked Glenn.

"We go out into the countryside and 'encourage' the volunteers to speed up mobilization," Glenn said with a smile.

"I'm guessing Master Sergeant Ricks is doing most of the encouraging," Diana said, smiling back.

"Yeah, we're just there for a show of force. He's such a force of nature that he hasn't had to do anything except show up and explain the law. To be honest, him just showing up is threatening. Griff doesn't really need us. But since we're on his shit list, we have to follow him around," Glenn said with a sigh.

Diana smiled and asked, "What did you do to earn his attention?"

Glenn sighed again and said, "A few of the boys got into a bar brawl with some other Guard members. To be honest, we deserve the extra work we've gotten. The only reason we were so close to Apple Valley when the GEMs invaded was because Griff had us climbing up and down the cliffs just east of Apple Falls. One of the many special training assignments designed to make his displeasure clear."

"Well, I guess I'm glad for the bar brawl then. I don't know what would have happened if your team hadn't shown up when they did," Diana said.

Glenn sat back on his elbows and asked, "How well do you know Tee Stone?"

Diana felt the question deep in the pit of her stomach. She suddenly felt guilty enjoying Glenn's company. Not because of Ansen, but because of Tee. A wide range of emotions cascaded through her mind until she realized she needed to answer his question. "Yes, I know him. We have known each other since elementary school."

"What can you tell me about him?" Glenn asked.

Diana looked down as she gathered her thoughts. She wasn't sure what to say. Clearly not that he was the most wonderful man she knew. That she was wildly in love with him. What would a member of the Guard want to know? She finally settled on, "He's very unusual. Everyone who knows him was as surprised as everyone else when he was selected for the Guard. But we weren't shocked. The surprise was that the Guard saw past his stature. He's a natural leader and highly intelligent. Apple Valley won the Pacifica capture-the-flag last year purely on Tee's abilities. He has a way of getting people to want to follow him."

Glenn clearly had questions he wasn't going to ask. Diana could tell he had seen the impact of his question. It was to his credit that he wasn't rude enough to put her on the spot. He only said, "I keep hearing impressive things about him. I'm looking forward to meeting him."

After a few moments Diana abruptly stood, said her goodbyes for the evening, and wandered back to her tent, clearly troubled. As she walked away, Glenn watched her with lots of unanswered questions held back.

CHAPTER 24

PEACE NEGOTIATIONS

Jennifer Malrey had avoided tabling the peace negotiations agenda for as long as possible. Mobilization was nearly complete. Eureka had been slow to comply, but had finally sent a reasonable contingent. She heard Master Sergeant Ricks had been sent to get them moving. She didn't want to know what his arguments were because she suspected it involved more than encouraging words.

The council's role in mobilization had faded to dealing with minor issues. Therefore, she could avoid it no further. Attempts had been made over the years to make peace with the GEMs and all had been disasters. A peace commission would be sent out and never heard from again. The last time a negotiations team had been sent out, some of them had been brought back on a moonless night and tortured within hearing of the Wall.

A Guard rescue team was immediately sent out. After a protracted melee in the dark, they returned with only the dismembered body parts from the male members of the peace commission. The GEMs had left it to their imaginations what had become of the two females. It was crazy to consider this. Jennifer had spent some time with Del a few days before trying to understand Councilman Barlow.

She had greeted him in her office saying, "Thanks for meeting with me, Professor. I'll be blunt and save both of us time. I try not to talk about council members behind their backs. But I'm having trouble understanding Councilman Barlow. I know he used to be a professor of history at the university, so I was hoping you could help me. My goal is to better understand him so I can make the council's agendas go more smoothly."

Del smiled grimly and said, "He can be a handful. In summary, he is brilliant, hardworking, and has a prodigious memory. His passion as a young scholar was the history of Pacifica, especially the decisions and events that led to our troubles with the GEMs. He knows the original colonists were committed pacifists, and he desires we return to those philosophies."

Jennifer wrinkled her brow and said, "An in-depth understanding of history would seem to me to be an attribute of someone with views completely the opposite of Barlow's."

Del nodded in agreement and said, "In my experience it's the brilliant who sometimes latch onto ideas and beliefs that defy logic. They know they are smarter than everyone else and so when they get off track, you can't bring them back. The basis of his defiance is his conviction that the official history of Pacifica has been systematically altered. He has created a compelling story based on a fairly substantial number of minor contradictions in the record. The history department is unified in believing this is simply the natural result of chaos from the Colony War and the collapse of civilization. Post-Colony War historians living in abject poverty took oral descriptions of events and wrote them down as history. As you might suspect, individual oral traditions, especially those several generations removed, are not considered dependable by serious historians. He claims the number and type of contradictions shows a clear intent to deceive."

"If he doesn't believe the official history, what does he believe?"

"Barlow believes that Ships 1 and 3 cheated the GEMs out of Pacifica. He believes this planet should have been left to the GEMs who were specifically altered to thrive here. We were supposed to emigrate to one of the more habitable planets in the sector. The basic story he's constructed has our ancestors breaking their word to Ship 2 and colonizing the peninsula with plans to conduct genocide on the GEMs. The surprise attack didn't work as planned and we got stuck here. He believes the GEMs have good reasons not to trust us and the current situation is the fault of our ancestors."

"Okay, this is starting to make some sense. Well, not literally. But it does explain some of his extreme statements and proposals. To be fair, he is very helpful on most topics that come before the council. As you said, he is intelligent and hard-working. He takes his role as councilman seriously and serves Eureka Valley citizens as best he can. He asks excellent questions, making us think critically about all aspects of our agenda items. I just wish the weird stuff would go away."

"There is little hope of that. I've spent many hours arguing with him when he was at the university. He would have become chair of the history department if he were a little more mainstream. He thinks I'm the one who blocked him, so I won't be much help trying to talk sense into him," Del said.

"Thanks for coming. The background helps. Let's keep this conversation between us. It will just make things worse if Barlow thinks I'm conspiring against him."

"Any time, Ms. President," Del said as he got up and strolled out of her office.

President Malrey brought the council to order and announced, "This morning's agenda is to discuss options for pursuing peace negotiations with the GEMs. Councilman Barlow has proposed assembling a negotiations team under his leadership and approach the GEMs in person. He desires the team to have the authority to negotiate with the GEMs under provisions agreed to by this council. Councilman Barlow, do you have anything to correct, clarify or add to the proposed agenda item?"

"Your description of the proposed agenda item is accurate, Ms. President. I would like to emphasize that my proposal has the council in complete control of decisions regarding any treaty or agreement we can obtain. I know some of you fear I might exceed my authority in discussions with the GEMs. I want to assure all of you I am in complete agreement with the importance of majority support for every aspect of negotiations."

"Are there any questions about the proposed agenda?" Jennifer asked. As she looked around the table, it was clear from the body language how this would go. Eureka would align around some sort of plan to offer peace to the GEMs while the other two regions would be reluctant to offer any concessions.

Councilwoman Ricks raised her hand. "Can we start with a discussion of what should be negotiated before we decide how to negotiate? Every peace team that has approached the GEMs in person has disappeared. Well, sometimes body parts come back. Consideration of safety for the negotiating team will need careful planning."

Jennifer was nodding as she said, "That seems reasonable. Let's vote on whether to start with the specifics of the negotiation. This only refines the order of discussion and voting, not the proposed agenda by Councilman Barlow. All in favor of the revised agenda, raise your hands."

Looking around the table, Jennifer smiled and said, "The agenda is approved with the first order of discussion and vote focused on an agreement of negotiation details. After we agree on what we want to concede, and what we want in return, we'll turn to how we will approach the GEMs." Jennifer once again looked around the table for head nods of approval and continued. "Councilman Barlow, you have given this more thought than anyone. Do you have a specific proposal or framework?"

Barlow smiled, looked around the table, and said, "Thank you, Ms. President, I do. I believe our goal ought to be a world where we live side by side without regard to genetic origins. GEMs ought to be our neighbors, not our enemies." Looking around the table, Barlow recognized the look of shock and horror on the faces of his fellow councilpersons. He held up his hands, palms forward, and said, "Not immediately, but over time. I think it's important to have a goal in mind."

Several voices broke in loudly, shouting over one another. "Come to order!" Jennifer said firmly, with steel in her voice. She was usually so soft-spoken that this unusual show of sternness shocked everyone into silence. Jennifer glanced around the table until it was clear everyone was in control of their emotions. She turned to

Barlow and said, "Councilman Barlow, could we stick with the agenda as it stands and delay a discussion of long-term goals for another time? I'm concerned the council will get off track and we won't make progress today."

Barlow grunted his agreement and said, "Okay, okay, we can dive into the specifics, but we need to get on the same page on where we want to eventually end up. Ignoring that for now, here is a list of concessions I believe we should make.

"One: turn the fresh water back on. A good-sized region of the continent used to get all its fresh water from what flows through Landfall Valley. With water turned back on, it opens up an area of land three times the size of the peninsula for agriculture. Dumping all that fresh water into the ocean is what our ancestors would have called a war crime.

"Two: encourage trade with the GEMs. We should set up a trading post in what are now Guard barracks and supply warehouses.

"Three: concede territory. There are several undeveloped valleys in the Apple Valley region. From the Guards report on the latest incursion, my understanding is that it's possible to bottle up the GEMs in these high valleys if problems arise. We owe them restitution for the wrongs of the past. Conceding territory should go a long way to convincing them we are finally acknowledging our responsibility for the horrible treatment they have endured."

There was stunned silence in the room. Councilwoman Ricks raised her hand and said, "May I be recognized?"

"You have the floor, Councilwoman," Jennifer

responded.

Ricks took a deep breath, clearly trying to gain control of her anger. She looked around the room and said, "I propose we take each of these points separately and vote on them. I also propose we start with a vote on item one, turning on the water. We can likely come to some sort of agreement on this and having success early will help the rest of the discussions."

Councilwoman Ricks once again impressed Jennifer. Ricks was clearly the unofficial leader of the council. She had a way of dividing up agendas and proposing votes that moved the council down the road she wanted it to take. It was like watching a chess master systematically orchestrating the game and controlling an opponent.

"Before we vote on your proposal Councilwoman Ricks, let hear from the rest of the council on whether they have additional concessions for consideration," Jennifer said, looked around the table and when no one raised their hand she continued. "Okay then let's vote on whether to discuss and vote on each proposal separately."

The entire morning went by with one heated discussion after another, with an occasional personal insult thrown in. Jennifer had been forced to stop the discussions several times to remind everyone of the council's engagement rules. She was exhausted. She felt like she had been walking a tightrope all morning.

Jennifer worried that the growing divisions between the regions risked pushing the council into dysfunction. Eureka Valley was often in conflict with both Apple Valley and Landfall Valley. The physical land size and population were equal to the combination of the other two valleys. They provided sixty percent of the food for Pacifica. They believed they ought to have more say in council decisions. Taking yet another deep breath, she said, "Let's review decisions from this morning's official notes and close off this agenda item. Here are the decisions from Councilman Barlow's agenda proposal.

"One: an offer to turn on fresh water will be made under the condition that all hostilities cease.

"Two: any hostilities after the water is turned on will result in it being turned back off.

"Three: if we still have peace five years after the water is turned on, we will offer to set up a trading post outside the Wall and on the other side of the dry moat.

"Four: GEMs will not be allowed past the boundary of the dry moat.

"Five: no land concessions will be made.

"Six: the offer of turning on fresh water in return for a long-term commitment of peace will be made in written form. Councilman Barlow will sign this treaty offer for the council. The Guard will construct a kiosk on the GEM side of the dry moat with the offer posted."

Barlow was visibly angry. He took a deep breath, let it out, and then said, "I am extremely disappointed in our inability as a council to consider a legitimate offer of peace. We are the ones responsible for the horrendous death and destruction on both sides. I am disappointed that we are not taking responsibility for our past actions. I understand the council has spoken and this agenda item is closed. However, before we break for lunch, I have an emergency agenda item for this afternoon's session."

"Go ahead, Councilman Barlow. What is your proposed agenda item?" Jennifer asked.

"I propose a vote of no confidence in President

Malrey," Barlow said, smiling smugly and looking directly at Jennifer. Turning toward the other councilpersons, he said, "She is not equipped to execute the duties of the Office of the president. Her incompetence in allowing full mobilization when no threat is apparent is proof of this. Her inability to shepherd the council to a responsible peace offer is further proof. The damage caused by her incompetence is serious enough to negate her ability to continue in her post."

Councilwoman Ricks shook her head from side to side. Clearly frustrated, she said, "President Malrey, would you mind stepping out while we discuss this? The constitution calls for us to convene in your absence for this process. We will first vote in a temporary head of the council, then discuss the proposal at length, and finally vote. We can call witnesses if necessary so this could take days, perhaps weeks, to execute. As you know, it will take a two-thirds majority to instigate a general election to select a new president. If the two-thirds vote is successful, the temporary head of the council will take over your responsibilities until an election can be held."

"Who made you leader of this?" Barlow asked hotly.

"Nobody. I'm going over the process so we can excuse the president from the meeting," Ricks said with her eyes boring into Barlow's. "We'll communicate progress as we work through this, Ms. President."

"Thank you, Councilwoman Ricks. I will comply with whatever the council needs from me throughout the process," Jennifer said as she stood, turned, and walked briskly from the room, clearly shaken.

Jennifer was sitting in her office late that afternoon thinking about the possibility of being the first president voted out in her first month in office. The newspapers and history books would have a field day if that happened. They would make much of the fact that she was the youngest president to be elected in the history of Pacifica. She knew she had made the right decisions, given the information she had. There was a lingering doubt whether Del had provided false information to her. She had watched him spin a completely made-up analysis to the council. If she didn't know it was false, she would have believed him completely."

Her door suddenly burst open and one of her aides came in, out of breath. "They're here!" he said.

"Who's here?" she asked, confused.

"GEMs! Thousands of them! They're setting up camp on the horizon," the aide said in a panic.

And just when I thought I had problems, Jennifer grimly mused.

As the aide back ran out, Councilwoman Ricks calmly walked in, her demeanor a welcome change. "It's done; you've been exonerated. The vote was five-to-one," she said, a little out of breath. "Once the GEMs showed up, the posturing and silly debating ceased. The accusation ended up being poor judgement in voting for full mobilization. We shot down the leadership in the peace process complaint as ridiculous since we did the voting with no tie breakers needed.

"The council's opinion now is that you may have saved us all. I don't know what Barlow was thinking, voting for no confidence. Doing that after a massive number of GEMs show up on our front door was not a good move politically. That rash act destroyed his credibility with the other council members. Even Councilwoman Rivers, who has consistently supported him, is disgusted."

"Thank you, Councilwoman. I assume they voted you temporary head?" Jennifer asked.

"Yes, the majority wanted this over quickly. I have a reputation for little to no patience," Ricks said with a smile.

Jennifer stood up, took a deep breath, and prepared herself to become a wartime president. "Well, let's go take a look at them," she said as she motioned Ricks to follow her up to the roof of the government building. From there, they would have a view beyond the Wall and discuss what needed to be done next.

CHAPTER 25

THE WALL
DAY 1

Tee and Jay stood on the Wall looking out over the downward sloping sandy plain below. The sun was just starting to rise with a thin angry red skyline. It was beautiful. The view and fresh new morning smell provided pleasure for Tee against the constant anxiety of the past few days. Thousands of tents with many thousands of GEMs were massed just outside the range of Pacifica's weapons. The only good news was they didn't appear to be forming up for an attack yet.

"I supplied water on the Wall when I was a boy," Jay said. "But I don't remember the number of GEMs ever being this massive."

"I heard Griff telling the CGG the same thing yesterday," Tee replied. "Griff was right to push hard for full mobilization. We wouldn't be in shape to defend the Wall right now if he hadn't."

"My dad told me the retired Guard has already been mobilized. He was asked to form an additional reserve squad for work below the Wall made up of retired Guard and second year Newbies," Jay said. "They're formed up and working on squad coordination exercises."

Tee and Jay continued to look out into the distance, lost in their own thoughts. Tee considered the Wall and its placement, deciding it was well thought out. The canyon below the dam had high cliffs on each side that were easily defended. That ended abruptly four hundred yards out. The belief was that the original colonists had intentionally sculpted them to create a killing field. Across this choke point was a twenty-yard-wide dry moat. It was deep and stretched across the entire width of the canyon. The moat was useful in slowing attacks and making it difficult for siege towers and other large war machines to be brought to the Wall.

The Guard Newbies in Tee's recruiting class had been formed up for Wall duty. They were another full training cycle, from being added to specialty veteran squads and platoons who might fight below the Wall. Tee was still smarting from being ordered to arm himself with his bow for this battle.

"I want you with your bow on the Wall, Tee. You're much more effective with that than with a spear. When you go below the Wall, it's a different matter," Griff said.

"Do I join one of the Wall Archer groups?" Tee said with frustration evident in his voice.

"No. You're going to stay with me as an aide. I'll be on the Wall much of the time directing squads and platoons or we'll be plugging gaps if the Wall is breached," Griff explained. "I want you to watch the battle develop. Let me know if you have any ideas that might gain us an advantage. If you think I'm making a mistake, I want to hear that too."

"If you go below the Wall, will I go with you?" Tee said with a hint of challenge in his voice.

Griff turned and locked eyes with Tee. "You'll do what I tell you to do," Griff said in a commanding voice, continuing to stare.

Tee just nodded and automatically said, "Yes, sir," acknowledging Griff's unquestioned authority.

Griff gave him a crooked, knowing look before turning away.

The "sir" had come out without thinking. It was like he was back in recruit training again. He knew better than to call a non-com, sir. Embarrassing. At least he hadn't saluted. Griff was scary, Tee thought. He was a collaborative leader much of the time. But when he gave an order in that voice, you simply obeyed without thinking about it.

Tee was pulled out of his thoughts by Griff, motioning him that they were moving to another section of the Wall. He stayed a couple paces behind as Griff stopped to give orders to various squads and 'suggestions' to the officers. When they got near the center gate, they ran into the Apple Valley archer unit. They arrived as his mother was instructing Tia on keeping the Wall Archers supplied with arrows.

"You stay seated next to the arrow stand, handing the archer arrows when requested. She will say 'arrow' and you will hand her one with the fletching toward her, but with the arrowhead pointing off to the side. We don't want any accidents where you get stuck with an arrowhead," Arti said.

"How will I know when to go get more arrows?" Tia asked.

"Count down how many arrows are left in increments of five. For the final group, count down each arrow as you hand it to the archer. Do you understand this part?"

"Yes. I count down. Twenty-five, twenty, fifteen, ten, five, four, three, two, and one," Tia said.

"Good. The archer will decide when you should go

down to the arrow bin for a new supply. Don't go down until she tells you to," Arti continued. "When you walk to the staircase, do not linger in front of the arrow slits. Keep yourself out of the direct line of an arrow or spear that might find its way through," Arti told Tia with Diana nodding in agreement just behind her.

Looking up as she finished her instruction, Arti noticed them standing there. She turned and smiled, saying, "It's a beautiful morning."

Griff grunted and lifted his hand to point out beyond the Wall and said, "I'm not sure how you see anything beautiful in that."

"My mother always insists on recognizing the good in a bad situation," she replied, hesitated, and with her smile brightening a bit said, "I admit it can be irritating at times."

"Well, wisdom can be irritating," Griff said with a grin. "I stopped by to request Diana be ready to lead the Apple Valley group. I would like to be able to have you move around to support other parts of the Wall if needed. I wouldn't ordinarily ask this, but I've seen her in action and know she can manage it."

Diana's face blushed, and she looked to the ground, embarrassed. Tee swelled with pride for Diana, knowing the truth in what Griff said.

"I agree she can handle it. How will I know if I'm needed elsewhere?" Arti asked.

"I'll send a runner with instructions. It may not happen. But I would like to be prepared for a situation needing your special skills," Griff said. As Arti nodded, an increase in noise from the GEM encampment reached them.

"Looks like they're forming up. Good luck today,"

Griff said, looking at them both. After they had walked a few paces away, Griff turned, grabbed Tee by both his shoulders and turned him so they were face to face. Pulling him close with an intense look in his eyes, he said in a low voice only Tee could hear, "Ad Victoriam."

Tee hesitated, surprised by what Griff said. Then, remembering, he responded saying, "Cum scuto aut in scuto."

It was an age-old private ritual of the Guard spoken in old earth Latin. It was said from a veteran to a Newbie as their first battle was about to begin. The veteran would say 'To Victory' and the Newbie would respond by saying 'With shield or on shield.' It signified the veteran believed the Newbie was required for victory. It meant the Newbie was willing to give his life to protect Pacifica. Tee had forgotten all about this ritual in the excitement. His breast swelled with pride at the honor of being addressed in this way by the Master Sergeant of the Guard. He was truly prepared to go forth and die for Pacifica and victory.

They walked down the wide staircase near the main gate and reviewed preparations for the Guard units staging for work below the Wall. Barin Phillips, Jay's father, was there with his reserve unit. He greeted them both warmly. Griff quizzed him on what he had done to prepare his hastily assembled reserve squad. He nodded approval at what had been achieved in so little time.

As they were walking away, Barin Phillips grabbed Tee's arm, pulled him off to the side and said quietly, "My son has a bunkmate to be proud of. Look out for him, Tee." Tee glowed with pride at that request. He knew everyone thought Jay protected him, not the other way around. He would indeed look out for Jay.

As they were completing the inspection, a roar erupted from beyond the Wall. Tee followed Griff as he briskly hurried back up the main staircase. They were just in time to see a full-scale assault begin to take shape. They noticed the peace offering kiosk burning brightly in the distance.

Tee watched as GEM teams carrying bridges ran up to the moat and placed their platforms across the opening. Catapults opened fire from behind the Wall and atop the cliffs to either side, dropping large stones on and just behind these structures. Many rows of women and older men fired coordinated flights of arrows to fall on the mass of GEMs queuing up to cross the bridges. While some bridges were destroyed, enough bridges survived to move a few thousand GEMs across the moat and into position to directly attack the Wall. Tee was appalled by the number of GEMs they were willing to lose just to stage an attack.

Then they came running full speed and screaming at the top of their lungs. Mixed in with the mass of GEMs attacking the Wall were scaling ladders. The Wall Archers concentrated on identifying experienced fighters associated with the ladder crews and taking them out. The early waves of attacks were oftentimes heavily populated with young warriors with a few gray beards to guide them.

"This isn't the serious assault, Tee," Griff said. "Notice the older warriors trying to organize the younger ones. This is simply an attack to give them experience and hopefully soften us up. The big push will start this afternoon or, if we're lucky, tomorrow morning. Their goal is to get us into a state of fatigue, eat up our supply of stones and arrows, and then attack with their best troops."

With this pronouncement, Tee had a sudden sinking feeling in his gut. He was intimidated. If this wasn't a serious assault, he wasn't sure he was prepared. After a few panicked moments, Tee shook off the fear and notched an arrow. He started picking off some of the older looking GEMs and battle fever took over. He replaced fear with grim determination. Tee would do whatever it took to defeat these devils or die trying.

Tee was surprised when Griff suddenly said, "Battle always starts with fear, Tee. Even for veterans. I can see you've overcome it. Not everyone does."

The rest of the day was pure exhaustion. Griff had boundless energy and Tee ran after him from section to section. Wherever the battle intensified or whenever the Wall was breached, they went into the middle of it. Twice scaling ladders had gotten set with enough time and support to get GEMs to the top. Both times Guard squads arrived to support the volunteers and throw them off. On one occasion, Tee glimpse a tired but whole Jay wiping off his sword only to have to turn around and head off in the other direction after Griff once more. He was thankful for that aspect of being Griff's aide. He had seen almost everyone he was worried about at some point in the day and knew, at least in that moment, they were safe.

As the sun was setting and the GEMs were retreating once more back across the moat, Griff turned to Tee and said, "That should be the last assault today. Did you notice when the quality of the warriors improved?"

"The third assault seemed more organized. It appeared to have less age gap between the warriors and their leaders," Tee observed.

Griff nodded in agreement and said, "They came early with their best warriors. This is either a good thing or a bad thing. It's good if they're running out of inexperienced warriors. It's bad if they have so many experienced warriors that they can send wave after wave with no letup," Griff said. "They haven't attacked at night for several decades. Nobody knows why. That makes me suspicious. If there is one thing I know about the GEMs, it's that they're patient, smart, and persistent."

Griff and Tee walked at a leisurely pace down to the Apple Valley archers' station. Griff got his mother's attention and asked, "Arti, do you have a watch supervisor schedule for the Wall Archers tonight?"

"Yes, Diana will take the first watch. Landfall and Eureka will provide supervisors for the second and third watches. We have an AC meeting after nightfall to discuss results from today and plans for tomorrow," Arti explained.

"Good, I'm going to have the volunteers keep torches lit all night every ten feet along the Wall. Please have the AC delegated night supervisors double check that the volunteers are keeping them lit during their rounds. I would like flare arrows every fifteen minutes or so. Make it random. Send out more if anything odd happens or someone hears something suspicious. Have them pay attention to the dead bodies. As you know, it's not unusual for GEMs to fake a death and try and sneak up the Wall."

"Will do," Arti said.

Griff motioned Tee over and said, "Go get something to eat, rest, and meet me here before sunrise tomorrow."

Tee was exhausted as he walked to the barracks. The sun had just set, and Jay was already there when he arrived. He looked drawn. "You okay, Jay?" Tee asked with concern in his voice.

"A couple of scratches, but mostly just tired. Spent the day warding off scaling ladders. Got in some close quarter work once when a ladder got set and GEMs reached the top. We eventually got it thrown back," Jay said. "How about you?"

"Exhausted. My arm, wrist, and fingers are sore from firing arrows. I don't think I've ever shot that many in one day before. The GEMs don't seem to care how many warriors they lose. However, when the leaders are taken out, they lose focus and eventually call a retreat," Tee said.

"What was Griff's impression?" Jay asked.

"You're not going to like it. He said he's never seen so many GEMs in reserve beyond the moat. He claims the fighting tomorrow will start to ramp up and become serious," Tee explained.

"That wasn't serious today? Really?" Jay asked. He hesitated and in a serious tone said, "Is he worried?"

"It's hard to tell, but I think he is. I don't think he's lost confidence in our ability to withstand whatever they throw at us. But I know he's disturbed by the number of casualties we're taking. I can tell my mom is worried. She hides it really well, but she can't hide it from me," Tee said.

"We'll break them tomorrow, Tee," Jay said, and Tee believed him.

Tee and Jay walked to the mess tent and had a quick dinner with Pete, Ansen, and Tia. Kale and Zeb joined them as well. With one exception, they were all visibly tired. The exception was Tia. Her bubbly, dramatic personality was in full swing. It was a needed tonic for them all. Tee sat back and listened to all the stories of the day. The excitement in their stories was mixed with fear, and it made him all the more determined. Family and good friends, what else could a man ask for in life?

As they headed back to the barracks Tee said, "I'm too wound up, Jay. I'm going to go walk a bit."

Diana found herself enjoying the quiet walk along the Wall in the early evening. It was warm, with a slight cool breeze blowing down from the dam above. She was glad the breeze was not coming from the opposite direction. The stench would be horrible. There were a lot of dead GEMs out there. Her duties were simple, which gave her time to think. Something that wasn't possible during the chaos of the past few weeks. She had decided before she left Apple Valley she was going to break it off with Ansen. But she would wait until after the battle. Ansen needed to concentrate on protecting himself on the Wall. Diana knew he'd be distracted if she had her talk with him now.

Once that was done, she was going to tell Tee how she felt about him. Tee had been rather cool to her since he was asked to join the Guard. If he didn't share her feelings, she would be devastated. What she did know was that she would only marry if she were truly in love with someone. Marrying Ansen would be logical. It could be a good life. But it would not fulfill her dreams and desires. She suspected it would not fulfill Ansen's either. Perhaps they both would have been disappointed.

Suddenly, Tee's voice came out of the gloom. "Diana." She flinched. "Sorry, did I surprise you?"

Diana's face heated, and she hoped it was dark enough that Tee didn't notice the blush. She felt like he had caught her thinking about him. "Yes, sorry, I was thinking about Ansen."

Oh God, why did I say that?

"He's okay. Saw him with Pete and Tia at the mess tent just a few minutes ago. He asked about you and I told him you were good at the end of the day. He was relieved. He told me to look out for you and Tia," Tee said in his earnest, caring manner.

Diana was still a little agitated with herself by the Ansen remark Tee had surprised out of her. "Are you okay?" she asked. Another stupid thing to say. They had talked briefly at the end of the day, and he already told her he was fine.

Tee looked a little confused but said, "Yeah, a couple scratches. Nothing to worry about. Are you sure you're okay?" he asked with clear concern showing in his voice.

"Yes, just distracted, I guess."

Oh God, do I ever stop saying stupid things? Now he'll think I'm referring back to Ansen again.

Then the conversation smoothly evolved into the calm, casual, and easy nature they had always had with each other. They walked along the Wall talking about home, people, Friday night bonfires, and hunting trips. The last topic transitioning into what they both would like to do when the battle was over.

"When this is over, I just want to go into the woods. Do a little hunting," Tee said with a wistful smile.

"That sounds absolutely wonderful. Let's go. I tried hunting with Ansen. It was a disaster," Diana said, laughing.

"Let me guess. He did a poor job of pretending to enjoy the woods. He never stopped talking. And he scared away the game," Tee said, smiling.

"Exactly," Diana said. She opened her mouth to say more, but then bit her tongue. She had come really close to telling him how she felt about him.

There was awkward silence for a moment and then Tee quickly changed to a safer topic. "How is our arrow monkey?"

"Really good. Better than I expected. She followed her orders exactly. We were worried she would linger on the Wall when it wasn't necessary. Or worse yet, poke her head up to look out of one of the arrow slits. Neither turned out to be a problem," Diana said with pride. "Have caught her early in the morning and late in the evening at the Guards' practice range. She's already a couple of years ahead of the other girls. You better watch out or she'll knock you off your perch."

Tee smiled and said, "I have little time to practice anymore. The Guard is keeping me busy doing other stuff. It relaxes me so I get out as often as I can."

"Oh, making your excuses ahead of time? You afraid you won't be able to keep up with me?" Diana said, falling into that easy banter she and Tee had always had.

"Yeah, you caught me," Tee said, smiling.

"By the way, I caught up with Hestie at Jay's mother's house. God, it was good to see her. I have missed her horribly since she left for university." Diana hesitated, then said, "I hope Jay is as over the moon about her as she is about him," Diana said with a hint of a question in her voice.

"I can't imagine her being any more smitten with him than he is with her. I'm really happy for both of them. And to save you from having to ask, yes, Jay really is a good guy. They're a good match, Diana," Tee said with his voice and face matching his words.

Diana had been watching Tee closely as he answered. She was vastly relieved by his answer. It surprised her how much that news relaxed her. She thought she knew how her best friend felt about him. A brother, not a lover. But with Ansen constantly trying to push the two together, she had begun doubting whether she really did understand their relationship. Well, perhaps paranoia was setting in now she had woken up and gotten honest with herself. What a relief to know she wouldn't have to deal with best friend jealousy.

They stayed on safe topics for the rest of her watch. Both losing track of time. Tee had a way of making her feel comfortable, warm, safe, and peaceful. He also excited her in a way no other man did. Diana wanted to drown in all of it. But that would have to wait.

CHAPTER 26

THE WALL
DAY 2

Tee was up extra early and decided to leave Jay alone to get a bit more rest. Last night Griff had told him to meet him on the Wall "Before sunrise." Tee hadn't asked what that meant. If there was one thing that irritated Griff, it was people being late. It gave Tee time to think.

He vividly remembered stumbling upon Diana the night before. He had stopped and watched her from the shadows before he announced himself. She was simply breathtaking. Tall and strong, with a heart of gold. Nobody was more beautiful in his eyes. His heart ached thinking about her.

Their discussion started off strangely. She was obviously worried about Ansen and distracted by it. He suspected she was sending him a message by bringing him up when Tee asked her how she was. Then the sudden enthusiasm to go hunting when all this was over. He was excited and troubled by it. She obviously didn't want Ansen along. Which made sense.

Tee smiled as he thought about how he had tried that once. It was easy to guess how it had gone for Diana. However, he wasn't sure how comfortable he would be alone with Diana. He might have to come up with an excuse to get out of it. Claiming Guard duties were wearing a little thin. Especially if he was given leave after the battle was over. It just hurt too much.

"Good morning, Tee," he heard Griff say from behind him.

Tee turned around and said, "Good morning."

"Thanks for getting here early. I wanted to discuss yesterday's battle before things heat up today. What did you learn?" Griff asked.

Tee straightened and gave his report, "The GEMs seem happy to trade lives for small gains. I don't think they place the same value on life that we do. The troops I saw yesterday morning were not very well trained. You mentioned they were the GEM version of Newbies. They didn't seem to have much weapons training or knowledge and experience on how to place and support their scaling ladders."

"Why would they waste inexperienced warriors this way?" Griff asked.

"I noticed our squads getting more and more aggressive as the day went on. Archers were exposing themselves more than they should as well. Maybe they are lulling us into a false sense of security they can take advantage of. They could also believe that sacrificing tens of GEMs for a few Pacifica warriors is worth it," Tee suggested.

"So, what do you suggest we do?" Griff asked.

"Tell everyone to be cautious, pay attention to changing capabilities, and stay defensive," Tee said.

"Good. That is exactly what everyone has been told to go over with their units," Griff said with a satisfied look on his face. "Pay attention to GEM squad cohesion when a leader goes down. They have trouble with coordination. Even at the squad levels, they are overly dependent on the squad leader."

"I did notice the squad coordination issue yesterday. I'll pay closer attention to larger scale moves today," Tee said, then hesitating he added, "How much trouble are we in?"

"Nothing we can't handle," Griff replied nonchalantly, turned, and strode off.

Tee took a deep breath and followed close behind. He was troubled. He made a habit of observing those around him. He was good at recognizing cues suggesting there might be more to the story. Griff didn't lock eyes with him when he responded. That likely meant he was anything but confident. He also noticed the volunteer reserves drilling in a phalanx formation yesterday afternoon. This was an integral part of the retreat plan to get as many people as possible back behind the dam if the Wall fell.

A multi-row phalanx with large square shields and long spears would set up and retreat step by step until it slowly dissolved back near the dam for the final run up the steep and winding dam road. In essence, it was a moveable Wall, slowing down the GEMs and providing an organized, purposeful retreat. Thinking about the phalanx sparked a thought he put away for later reflection as he noticed GEMs starting to cross the moat bridges and form up. The day had begun.

After the sun had gone down, and Griff finished his squad leader reviews, Tee walked back to the barracks. He saw Jay sprawled out on his bunk, looking spent. There were a number of bandaged wounds, but nothing that looked serious.

"Looks like you're not dead yet," Tee said, trying to joke.

"It's not from lack of trying, Tee," Jay said, not cracking a smile. "It was insane today."

"Seriously, are you okay?" Tee asked in a concerned tone.

"I'll have a few new scars to impress the girls, but nothing that will keep me out of the fight tomorrow," Jay said.

"Saw you fighting alongside Ansen during a Wall intrusion late afternoon," Tee said.

"Yeah, our squad came up in support when the GEMs made the Wall. Ansen and some of the other Apple Valley volunteers were doing a good job of keeping them confined, but it was a standoff. Ended up teaming with Ansen on an attack to break through. It was pure chaos. Waded in with sword and round shield, killing everything I saw," Jay said with a weary voice. "Your cousin is a good fighter, Tee."

"And a good guy as well," Tee responded.

"How about you? You look like hell," Jay asked with a forced grin.

"Similar story, a few minor wounds, but nothing serious. I spent the day chasing Griff around again. When he wasn't moving, I was taking out GEMs with my bow. Shooting fish in a barrel. I showed up with Griff toward the end of the same Wall infiltration you stopped and helped with. Griff was amazing. I know where all the crazy stories about him come from. They're all true," Tee said with admiration.

Jay nodded, adding, "He came charging in from the other side mowing them down and just like that the fight for control of the Wall was over. Then he calmly wiped his blade on a GEM tunic and told us all to get back to our stations. Next thing I knew, he was off down the Wall with you running after him."

"He never stops," Tee said.

"We lost a lot of Guard today. I've been asked to backfill a reserve squad tomorrow for duty below the Wall," Jay said with fire in his eyes. "And no, it won't be my father's squad. They don't put family members in the same squads for obvious reasons."

"They are backfilling Wall positions with some of the older youth reserve. My cousin Pete has been called up. He's thrilled and I'm worried. He's a good fighter, but he's immature," Tee said with visible anxiety.

"They'll put him with a seasoned veteran, Tee. Major Richards knows how to blend in the young and inexperienced."

They chatted for a while about inconsequential things, which calmed them both down. Then Tee said, "Go ahead and meet the others for dinner without me. I have to go find Griff. He told me if I have any ideas to let him know."

"Another suicide mission?" Jay asked, smiling.

"I hope not," Tee said grimly, smiling back.

Tee went to Griff's private bunk room and when he didn't find him there wandered around the encampment. He found Griff deep in conversation with the CGG and some of the other officers at a side table in the officer's mess hut. He couldn't interrupt that group, so he waited until they all filtered out. Griff saw him hanging around just outside the door and beckoned him in.

"Do you have something for me, Tee," Griff said.

"You asked me to tell you if I had any ideas. Is this a

good time?" Tee asked tentatively glancing over at the CGG.

"Go ahead, let's hear it," Griff said, nodding in encouragement.

"I noticed the GEMs throw everything into the kill zone quickly to try and overwhelm the Wall with numbers. When that starts to slacken, we counterattack, and they retreat just as quickly back over the bridges they installed. They seem to be very good at knowing when to retreat to avoid mass casualties. They are using the moat for defense in the same way we use the Wall," Tee said and looked at them both.

"Agreed, go on," Griff said while the CGG nodded his agreement.

"If we can trap them between the Wall and the moat just as they call for a retreat, we can hurt them," Tee explained.

"Yes, but how do we cut off their exit back over the bridges?" Griff said. His face was drawn gray from the long day.

"Jay Phillips has a friend whose father owns a warehouse storing this winter's heating oil for Landfall and Eureka Valleys," Tee said. "The cliffs on both sides of the canyon that butt up against the moat are sheer. If we build ramps on both sides, we can quickly roll barrels of heating oil down into the moat. They will break when they hit the bottom. There are trails from Landfall City to the top of both cliffs. They are just wide enough for carts, so getting the barrels there shouldn't be a problem.

"The GEMs don't pay much attention to the cliffs on either side, other than to stay far enough away to avoid getting rocks thrown down on them. If we quickly drop them at the right time, we might be able to get enough heating oil in the moat that, when lit, will trap them between the Wall and the moat. While they are confused by the moat being on fire, the Guard goes out and clears enough room in front of the Wall to have the Volunteers form up their phalanx. Then we drive them into the moat."

The CGG and Griff looked at each other, dumbfounded. Nobody had ever thought of setting the moat on fire. It seemed so obvious now. Turning the phalanx from a defensive weapon to its original purpose as an offensive one was inspired. The CGG looked at Tee and said, "What if we can't get enough heating oil in the moat to create a barrier?"

"Then we just do what we normally do when they retreat. We don't show the phalanx. If it doesn't work, we haven't lost anything other than having a colder than usual winter," Tee said.

Griff smiled, thinking that it really wouldn't matter to Apple Valley, since they burn wood for heat in the winter. "Give us a few minutes to discuss this, Tee." He flicked his hand toward the door and Tee exited the mess tent.

When they were alone, Griff said, "It's brilliant, Nate. And we don't have a prayer otherwise. Assembling and organizing the Phalanx is needed, anyway. If it doesn't work, we start the retreat to the dam."

Nate quickly shook his head in agreement and said, "Let's do it. We're out of options. It's clear we're going to be forced to retreat beyond the dam. It's a question of when not if." Nate hesitated and then said, "I have to admit Tee is impressive. The creativity he showed in training seems to translate to the battlefield. You were right, the Guard needs more people like him, regardless of stature."

"I'm afraid Tee might be unique. I'm starting to think he's the most dangerous man in Pacifica," Griff said, smiling. He then turned to walk out, stopped, turned back, and said, "Tomorrow I'm going to tell Tee he's your personal aide in case of a full retreat. He'll be very unhappy about not being in the fight. But if this plan doesn't work, we'll need some other crazy scheme to save us."

Tee was thinking about Diana and how to handle his next hunting trip when Griff walked out of the tent. He locked eyes with Tee, grinned and said, "Let's go get Jay and find his friend."

CHAPTER 27

THE WALL
DAY 3

It was another angry red skyline that greeted Tee and Jay early the next morning. They had been up all night on the special project. Unlike the confidence they felt the morning before, this was a somber morning. Pacifica's defense had been badly mauled. The veterans were voicing confidence to the Newbies, but you could tell it wasn't heartfelt. Pacifica could not continue to sustain the level of casualties they had been experiencing. The GEMs didn't seem to care how many casualties they suffered.

The day started much as it had the previous two days. The early assaults were mostly young males with limited fighting skills. These were mass assaults intended to soften up and tire the defense. As these waves of GEMs were cut down, experienced warriors started appearing, and the fighting got more intense.

Midafternoon Tee saw Jay below the Wall in a squad led by Dee, of all people. Tee still harbored some resentment of Dee. But he was glad to see that Jay was in a squad whose leader was known to be excellent. There was a reason he was in charge of recruit training.

Just then, disaster struck. Barin Phillips's squad of retired Guard and second year Newbies had successfully disabled a siege tower before it could get to the Wall. It was burning brightly. However, they were getting cut off from their retreat route.

Griff immediately sent a runner for Arti. He turned to Tee and said, "Stay here, organize the archers to focus on carving a path for Phillips's squad back to the Wall. Griff then disappeared down the stairway.

Arti, Diana, and a few of the Apple Valley archers showed up running with Tia and another arrow monkey trailing them. The two girls' arms were piled high with arrows.

Tee pointed to the Phillips squad situation and said, "We need to carve a path back to the Wall."

Arti yelled out in a firm voice, "Beth, Silvia, focus on taking out as many as you can between the squad and the Wall." Turning to Tee and Diana, she said, "Tee take the left and Diana take the right. Take the pressure off those flanks so they can focus on a retreat. I'll focus on the front. Tia with me."

And with that, a hail of arrows greeted the GEMs attempting to surround and consume the Phillips squad. It felt like the practice range and another of his mother's crazy scenarios again. In a way, it was comforting. His confidence in his mother was complete. Some in the Guard would have been outraged to be given orders by an Archer, especially their own mother. But Tee knew the best person to be in charge was giving the orders.

It was a gut punch when Tee saw Barin Phillips take a spear. He had been gaining confidence they would pull this off when Jay's dad was suddenly struck down. The squad was now leaderless, and it showed. As their formation crumbled, Dee came roaring in like an angry bear, Jay right on his heels. GEMs went down like bowling pins; Dee got them formed up properly again and hope reemerged. Jay went to check on his dad, but Dee shook his head sadly and motioned him to get back to fighting.

The GEMs recognizing Dee's leadership focused everything on overwhelming him. Recognizing the dire situation, Dee motioned Jay to lead them back to the Wall. Then he plunged headlong into the heart of the attack. When Dee went down, Jay countermanded the retreat order and led the squad back, clearing space around the badly wounded Dee. As Jay's squad floundered, Griff rushed out of the gate with Kale, Zeb, Moose, and Rilla. The GEMs were introduced to hell.

"You." Griff pointed at one of the less effective Newbies. "Grab Dee's collar and drag him along inside our formation until we get to the Wall. Jay, you're with me on the front line. Squad, retreat together one step at a time on my cadence."

Tee was amazed to see the GEMs leery of attacking Griff. Not that they didn't have good reason for caution. After the initial carnage, they stayed clear of him and focused their attack on the sides and back of the formation. Now that the squad was organized and tightly bunched, the effectiveness of the archers improved.

Under Griff's direction, the squad was soon in close enough proximity of the Wall for additional spearman to be sent out to help. The retreat path was cleared. Looking up now that his archery skills were no longer required, Tee saw that the area between the Wall and the moat was black with GEMs. These were the experienced ones, their best. The influx of GEMs crossing the bridges was starting to wane, so Tee rushed down to find Griff. It was time to prime the moat.

When he got down the stairs, he saw Dee on a surgical

table with Dr. Espers looking at Griff and shaking her head slightly side to side. The nonverbal message was clear: Dee wasn't going to make it. Griff went to Dee, bent down, and said something in a low voice. Dee, noticing Tee approaching, motioned him over and grabbed his tunic. He pulled him down close and, wincing in pain, he whispered, "Ad Victorium."

Shocked, it was all Tee could do to mumble back, "Cum scuto aut in scuto."

Dee nodded, smiled with a grimace, turned toward Griff, and grabbed his tunic to pull him close. "Take care of my boys for me Griff," he said, pleading in a barely discernible and whispery voice.

Griff locked eyes with him and softly said, "That's a promise old friend." With Griff's promise, and acknowledgment of friendship in hand, Dee died with a peaceful expression on his face.

Tee was shocked at this version of Dee. He had just given Tee the ultimate acceptance. No time to think about that now, Tee thought. He hated to interrupt but with tears threatening his own eyes he said in a clear voice, "Griff, it's time." Griff turned toward him with eyes shining. Tee saw Griff had a serious gash on his shield arm. It had been hastily wrapped with a blood-soaked bandage, but clearly needed some attention.

"Sit down. Take something for the pain. And let me sew that up," Dr. Espers interrupted.

"Work on those who really need it," Griff said.

"I make the medical decisions, Sergeant, not you," Dr. Espers said in a firm voice.

"Follow me to the top of the Wall. You can sew it up there. Save the pain medicine for the others," Griff said.

Tee had never seen Quinn and Hestie's mom back

down from anyone. But she just nodded, grabbed some antiseptic and bandages, and, with sewing gear in hand, followed him up the stairs.

When they got to the top, Tee pointed at the bridges and said, "It looks like they are gambling everything on this assault. The bulk of their experienced units appear to be on this side of the moat."

Griff turned to a runner and said, "Inform the CGG that it's time to signal the drop and form up for the attack."

As Dr. Espers was stitching up his arm, he stepped forward to look up and down the length of the Wall. "Stay still a minute," she ordered in a brisk voice.

Amazingly, Griff complied and, turning his head toward Tee, said, "They aren't going to call a retreat. They have the advantage, and they know it. Here are your orders. Light the moat when the barrels have all been dropped, or if it doesn't light, retreat. The CGG will come up here after we're formed up below. You are going to be his aide in case of a full retreat from the Wall. He will listen to your suggestions. Is that understood?"

"Yes," Tee said.

"I know you want to join us in the assault. You are capable. But you can make a bigger contribution by following orders," Griff said, then he turned and hurried down the staircase.

Tee could see the barrels dropping in quick succession on both ends of the moat. Either the GEMs hadn't noticed, or they were unable to get orders to their troops to retreat. It was amazing, but the bridges still had GEM units trickling over the bridges toward the Wall. He would have thought they could smell the fumes by now.

The CGG was standing next to him when the first fire

arrow disappeared into the moat. A satisfying whoosh was heard, and the moat quickly became a flaming inferno. Flames were shooting fifty feet above the top. The gates opened and defenders poured out of all the gates. Only a skeleton crew was left behind. The CGG had asked for volunteers to join the Guard in an all-out final assault below the Wall. In true Pacifica fashion, almost all men of fighting age signed up.

As predicted, when the moat erupted in flames and the gates opened with an all-out mass assault, the GEMs panicked. They shrank back away from the Wall, bunching together so tightly they couldn't fight effectively. A few of the more senior GEM squads recognized the situation and tried to disrupt the formation of the Phalanx. However, with the entire Guard below the Wall, it wasn't coordinated well enough to make a difference. The Phalanx formed quickly and started a determined march, spears forward, driving toward the moat. The GEMs hadn't seen long spears or large shields before. The Phalanx was completely foreign to them. They had no idea how to combat it. The key was keeping a tight formation. All the training done to retreat in this formation turned out to be good practice in moving forward as well. Some GEMs tried climbing the cliffs and a few even tried running back over the burning bridges. Tee had seen Griff with Jay at his side spearheading the initial assault to clear space for the Phalanx to form up. Then he spotted Pete in one of the back row slots in the Phalanx. This really was an all-out gamble when young boys were fighting below the Wall.

It soon became clear that their gamble was paying off. The GEMs were getting impaled on spears or being pushed by those trying to avoid the spears into the burning inferno of the moat. The Phalanx continued its methodical drive into the massed GEMs and what had been a fight turned into a massacre.

Tee guessed it would be a while before the GEMs would try another assault. He took a deep breath, and his muscles started to relax. A thin smile formed on his lips. Suddenly a spear flew past, threading its way between himself, the CGG, and Diana. Tee heard it hit something with a wet splat. Before he could register what had happened, he heard Diana scream in anguish. Turning, he saw an image he would never be able to extinguish from his mind.

Lying on the stone parapet, in a pool of blood impaled by the spear, was Tia. Looking quickly back in the direction the spear had come from, he saw Angus sprinting away toward the staircase

CHAPTER 28

THE WAGER

Grant was infuriated. He had been giddy with excitement at his certainty of a big score. He had bragged about it for three days to the other members of the survey crew. He even boasted to everyone and anyone who would listen on the feeds. He was a laughingstock now. Worse, this had been his opportunity to pay off the horrendous gambling debts he had accumulated. The odds makers had predicted true humans were more likely than not to survive this latest battle. It was clear now they had set the odds correctly. The odds being given for the true humans getting overwhelmed on the next attack by the mutants weren't attractive. The true human's days would soon be over. Grant needed to win back some of his losses. He knew thinking like this wasn't logical. But he just couldn't help himself. His luck would change.

CHAPTER 29

HALL OF HEROES'

The Hall of Heroes' was a large stately granite building in the center of an expansive and meticulously manicured park. It was located on a flat knoll above Lake Landfall, across from the capital. It was situated with its large bronze front doors looking out over the Landfall Lake dam. There was a sweeping view of the Wall and beyond. It was the final resting place for anyone who died in battle protecting Pacifica. Above its entrance read 'Semper Vilgilantes.' Always Vigilant.

Inside the building was an auditorium reserved for funerals and events to honor those who gave the ultimate sacrifice. The rest of the building consisted of hundreds of rooms big and small. They were each dedicated to the year those interned had given their lives. All Pacifica citizens were cremated upon death. The rooms had enclosed shelves with clay pots holding the ashes of the deceased. Some of the jars were empty. If they were of the Guard, their final insignia was attached to the pot. Everyone had a small plaque with their name and a short message. These messages were sometimes composed by the person whose ashes were being displayed and sometimes by close relatives.

Tee and Jay were standing in front of Tee's father's jar. The message said simply 'For us all.' Arti explained to Tee when he was young that they knew what a wonderful husband and father he had been. The message was to remind ourselves and others that this sacrifice was made for everyone, not just his family.

"How much do you remember about your dad, Tee?" Jay asked quietly.

"A little. I just remember being happy when he was around. My uncle really helped after he died by including me in all their family activities. He treated me like a son and still does. My father was his partner in their blacksmith business. He introduced my mom to my dad, so lots of history there," Tee said.

Jay just nodded and stayed by Tee's side until he was ready to go. They were there for Dee's funeral. It had been a full week of funerals. They had attended more of them than they could count. The Guard had been decimated. They heard recruiting was going to be increased with many more graduates than usual, given the situation. In fact, some of the recruits who had failed the cut based on points in the past two recruiting classes were being retroactively added. They were now in the Guard for life.

Tee and Jay had been close friends before the battle. But this joint experience added a bond that would never break. Tee was there for Jay, mourning his father. Jay was providing the same support as Tee mourned Tia. As they walked toward the auditorium, the hallway was quickly filling up. They were just able to find a seat before the ushers placed a rope across the door behind them and let everyone know they could listen from outside in the hall.

This funeral started the same as all the rest. The Guard chaplain got up and read verses, extolling the virtue of sacrifice. They were reminded that time on Pacifica was short and a better future with reunion was in store. After a blessing, he asked if there was a spokesperson from the family who would like to say a few words.

To everyone's surprise, Griff got up and walked to the front. All the Guard members looked at each other with an unspoken 'I didn't know Griff and Dee were related.' Tee had gotten to know Griff pretty well over the past two weeks. While outwardly he was his usual confident self, he looked a little shaken to Tee.

Griff stood up next to the displayed urn and said, "I am not related by blood to Dee. But I am nonetheless a brother. Both of Dee's grandfathers, his father, and three younger brothers are all interned here. They were all of the Guard and died protecting Pacifica. His mother died of a heart broken by war. Few families have given so much. His only remaining family was the Guard. Many of you are here today because he forced you to be better than you could have ever imagined. His passion was to develop raw recruits to reach their full potential. He did this because he cared deeply for each and every one of you.

"For this, he is widely reviled and disliked. He accepted this as a fair tradeoff. If he could help ensure a Guard member would go home to his family, he was happy to be cursed at the dinner table for it. He thought of every recruit as one of his boys. I know it doesn't fit with the image he presented. But he loved all his boys. He died saving them. I have nothing but admiration for Dee's commitment to the best traditions of the Guard. Sleep well, my friend. I'd pray for your admittance to heaven, but I know you're already there."

With that, Griff picked up the urn and, per tradition, carried it to the new room and placed it in its cubicle. Tee and Jay waited until the crowd thinned down to go in and pay their respects. It took quite some time. Written on his plaque was the message 'For the boys.'

"I guess you never really know a person, huh?" Jay said to Tee as he wiped his eyes. "If someone told me I'd be shedding tears over Dee, I would have told them they were crazy."

Tee nodded slowly in agreement and said, "I remember him crashing into that crowd of GEMs. He saved half the squad by doing that. Most of them Newbies. He easily could have followed standard doctrine. I hope I can be that brave if I'm ever in that situation."

"Do you mind if I take a few minutes by my dad's urn again?" Jay asked.

"Of course, I'll come with you. Take all the time you need," Tee said.

Jay's father's memorial had been tough. In addition to feeling horrible for Jay, it brought back memories of his own father's death. Jay ended up giving the memorial because his mother just couldn't. She had broken down during the ceremony and leaned over into Arti's arms and sobbed quietly. It was heartbreaking. His mother was staying at the Phillips home. When she was invited, Arti told Pam, "I don't want to intrude on your family during your grief."

Pam dried her eyes and said, "You understand, Arti. You've been through this. I need your strength right now if you can give it."

"Of course," said Arti.

Later that day, when Pam learned of Tia's death, she admonished her, saying, "Arti, you've been sharing my grief. It isn't right for you to keep me from doing the same for you." And after that, they sat and talked quietly for hours.

Tia's funeral was by far the worst. It was one thing to

accept that a fully grown man or woman fighting to protect Pacifica had given their life. But to accept that a child had died just seemed unnatural. Tee was in a fog during the ceremony. His Uncle Hugh had gotten up and talked about how happy and joyful Tia was. How she livened up everyone she came into contact with. How she was loved by everyone who knew her. Drying tears, he changed tone and said he had something to get off his chest. This part Tee would remember.

"There are those who say my sister should not have had a child on the Wall. They are wrong. Tia's passion was to be a Wall Archer, like her aunt. She died as a Wall Archer. She was killed by a deranged coward who should have been out fighting in the final battle with the GEMs. Arti loved Tia as much as I do, as much as her mother does. Do not dishonor Tia's name with these ridiculous accusations. Tia died as a Wall Archer, protecting us all."

After his uncle and aunt walked the urn to its final resting place, they all gathered in the hallway.

"Dinner tonight at my house?" Jay asked.

"It's really nice of your mother to include all of us. Are you sure this is okay?" Tee said.

"My mom is better when she has people she likes around her. She has really taken a liking to your mom. Feels she understands her and the pain of losing a husband. It's also important to her that she is there for your mother. She told me that losing a niece is just as bad or worse. She enjoyed meeting Diana, Ansen, Quinn, and especially Hestie. Believe me, this will be good for her," Jay said.

"Your mother actually asked my mom about Hestie. She was trying to ask whether she was a good person without insulting anyone," Tee said with a smirk.

"She didn't!" Jay said in mock horror, and they both laughed. A pleasant change from the past few hours.

"My mom told her you couldn't find a sweeter, more loving person," Tee said.

Arti walked over to them, and Tee asked, "Where's Ansen?"

"He showed up at the Phillips house late last night. He's having an especially tough time accepting Tia's death. He won't talk to anyone about it and is angry all the time. I'm getting worried," said Arti.

Tee saw Ansen, Diana, and Hestie off to the side. Ansen did indeed look angry. He left Jay and walked over. "I'm so sorry about Tia Ansen," Tee said.

"You should be!" Ansen shouted. Everyone in the hall stopped what they were doing and looked to see what was going on. "I warned you about him. You knew what he was capable of. He blames you for not getting into the Guard and for his dad being in jail. I asked you to look out for her while she was on the Wall. You said you would take care of her. Well, you didn't, and now she's dead."

Diana grabbed Ansen's arm and pulled him away, speaking softly to him. She then turned and frowned at Tee. She blames me too, thought Tee. With tears running down his face, he turned and walked briskly out into the gardens and disappeared.

Jay was the one who found him. He had to stop and think about what would make Tee comfortable and then headed to the grove of trees on the far edge of the gardens. As predicted, Tee was sitting in the middle of a mini forest. "Hey buddy, you okay?" Jay asked with concern.

Tee looked up at him for a few moments, looked back

down and said, "I should have been keeping better track of Angus. I knew he was looking to get even. Ansen is right, Tia's death is as much my fault as it is Angus's. I wish I had been the one to take the spear."

"That's crazy talk, Tee," Jay said. "It's not your fault a coward threw a spear at your back and missed."

"I appreciate you saying that, Jay, but it isn't true. Tia's death is on me." Tee hesitated for a few moments and then said, "Would you do me a favor?"

"Anything, Tee," Jay responded softly.

"Tell my mom and the others I'm going hunting. Ask them to leave me alone for a few days."

"I'll come with you if it would help," Jay said.

That drew a short-lived smile from Tee. It extended briefly to his eyes, then he said, "That's quite the sacrifice. I know how much you despise 'wandering around aimlessly in the woods.' Thanks, but it's best if I'm alone for a few days."

With that, Tee stood up and walked out of the Hall of Heroes' gardens alone with his anguish

CHAPTER 30

SOLITUDE

It had taken a few days, but Tee finally felt somewhat like himself again. He had done very little hunting. Just enough to fill his belly. His father taught him to kill only when you planned to eat it. So, he mostly hiked through areas he had never explored before. He was there for that sense of peace he got from being outdoors. It was a bit cold for camping in the open. So, he built a lean-to out of branches stacked up against a rock wall. He buried the frame under a thick blanket of fallen leaves.

At night, he brought heated rocks into his temporary home. It was cozy. He loved camping in the woods. In his opinion, this was not the hardship many others thought it was. Jay, in particular, would hate it. Diana would love it. This was where he could always find peace. Solve any problem. He had finally accepted the terrible events of the past two weeks and was ready to go back to real life.

His relationship with Ansen and Diana was never going to be the same. He had taken on the responsibility for looking after Tia and failed miserably. The look Diana had given him confirmed she agreed with Ansen. They were both good people and would forgive him in time. But it would never be the same.

Tee packed everything up, made sure the fire pit was

stone cold, and set off down the trail toward Apple Valley. He tried to clear his mind. But he kept coming back to the mistakes he had made and the things he should have done differently. Grammy had warned him that everything he valued in life could vanish in an instant.

"That is why you enjoy every moment, good or bad," she always said. It had been difficult to enjoy anything the past few days. Today, however, was a bit brighter than yesterday. He knew he would survive this. He had responsibilities. Pacifica still needed protection. Perhaps he would be like Griff and Dee. Never marrying. Making the Guard his family and his life. He had a future, even if it wasn't the one he had hoped for.

Tee's hunting senses suddenly kicked in and he stopped. The forest was too quiet. He notched an arrow and turned slowly around, trying to sense if anything was there. He wasn't overly concerned. Animals rarely attacked humans. But he was always cautious when out by himself. Suddenly, he felt a sting in his neck. He reached up, pulled something out, and looked at it. It was a small dart. His vision blurred. He heard something behind him and, turning, saw two small men cautiously coming out of the woods, fear clearly on their faces. As he collapsed on the ground, his last conscious thought was saying, "What odd clothing."

Tee woke up without opening his eyes. 'What to do if you're captured' was required training for all Newbies. Tee and Jay had wondered why they spent any time on this as GEMs were known to immediately torture and kill anyone they got their hands on. Lying quietly on some sort of soft surface, he controlled his breathing and listened intently.

The air smelled faintly like antiseptic, and the light

coming through his eyelids was harsh. He decided he hadn't been captured by GEMs. The two small men didn't look anything like GEMs. They looked like tiny Pacifica men. There really wasn't a reasonable explanation. There was someone else in the room, perhaps eight feet or so past his feet. Tee could hear him breathing and every once in a while he talked to himself in a low voice. The discussion he was having with himself was laced with obscenities.

A door opened somewhere to his right. It had a metallic sound, somewhat like the bronze doors at the Hall of Heroes. It was a sharper sound, however, and unfamiliar to Tee.

"Has the gorilla woken up yet?" asked a voice in a commanding tone. This voice belonged to whoever had just walked in the door. A foul odor came along with him.

"No boss, he just lays there quietly," said the voice just past his feet. Boss was said sneeringly and clearly intended as an insult.

"Don't sass me, Theo, or I'll make sure you end up in the mines instead of the Arena," said the commanding voice.

"You can stop with the empty threats. I know I have value, or I wouldn't be in one of these special cells," he said, but with the sneer gone. "You have to admit you wouldn't be too happy if our places were reversed."

"True enough. Don't give me any trouble and I won't go out of my way to make your life even more miserable. Help me out when I ask for it and I'll see you get some privileges," said the voice of the person Tee now thought of as Smelly.

"Deal. I'll pound on the Wall when he wakes up," said Theo.

The door opened and closed again. The foul smell started fading.

"Bastard! If I get my hands on you, I'll make you wish you'd never been born," Theo muttered and went back to being quiet.

The Arena? The mines? It didn't make any sense. After a few minutes, Tee decided he wasn't going to learn anything more by pretending to be asleep. He also didn't want to alert them he'd been faking it. Smelly must know how soon the drug in the dart would wear off and had come expecting him to be awake. Delaying any longer would cause suspicion. His training emphasized hiding all skills and capabilities unless a high probability of escape or death presented itself. He had to be submissive.

"Do not look your captors in the eyes. Hunch over, look at the floor, show fear," his instructor had said.

Tee opened his eyes and sat up. He looked up at Theo, forcing a fearful expression, scooched back against the Wall behind him, and cowered.

"Big as a barn, but acting like a little girl," Theo said with disgust in his voice. "What's your name, pussy?"

"Th-Theron, ah, sir," he said, affecting the voice and mannerisms of someone mentally challenged. Tee was proud of his last second addition of "sir."

Theo laughed maliciously and pounded on the Wall next to him.

Tee took a moment to glance around the area while mostly keeping his eyes locked on the floor. He was in a jail cell with bars for two of the four walls. Four cells were arranged in the corners of the room with just over two arm spans of distance between them. Only two of them were occupied. They each had a narrow bed, a toilet, and a sink. A guard came through the door on the opposite side of the two occupied cells.

"He's awake," said Theo.

"No shit, moron," said Smelly.

"I hope he's not earmarked for the Arena. If so, you guys screwed up," Theo said and laughed.

"What do you mean? He's from Pacifica. They'll love him in the Arena," Smelly said.

"Just talk to him. Says his name is Theron," Theo encouraged.

"Tell me about yourself, Theron," Smelly said with suspicion in his voice.

"I want to go home," Tee said, enunciating each word carefully. "Mom said to hike up to the lake and back before nightfall. She said she would have sweets for me when I get back," Tee said with his mouth partially open and a vacant scared look in his eyes.

Smelly broke out laughing. "Someone is dead over this. The bribes to get even one of these monsters from Pacifica must be astronomical." Smelly hesitated, scratched his head, thinking, and then said, "Oh well, he's still worth something. Maybe they can have one of the emperor's family members fight him in the Arena to show how tough they are."

"I'd enjoy slowly carving pieces off him. There would be lots of crying and screaming. I could make it really entertaining," Theo said with a sadistic grin.

Smelly ignored him, turned around, and exited out the door. Tee clearly heard it lock.

Theo then entertained himself by explaining to Tee all the painful and humiliating things he would do to him if there weren't bars between them. Tee curled up in a ball and whimpered. He had trouble staying in character because he couldn't believe the callousness and pure evil of the man. To abuse someone who had been born with mental challenges was about as low as a human being could get. Eventually, Theo tired of the harassment, which gave Tee time to review what he had learned.

He was no longer on Pacifica. Tee had trouble just grasping that concept. It meant their planet had been discovered. Whoever discovered it was practicing slavery but having to bribe someone to capture slaves on Pacifica. He was destined for the Arena, whatever that was. Given the comments, it sounded like some sort of blood sport. Just when he thought life couldn't get any worse, it had.

CHAPTER 31

IMPROVING THE ODDS

Grant's confidence was back. It wasn't often you could improve the odds. Even by a little. What he had done was surely illegal. But there was no way he would get caught. Grant had figured out that Guard member Theron Stone was the one who came up with the idea resulting in the defeat of the mutants. He discovered this by accident as part of his job as an anthropologist. He kept it to himself. He didn't log the files, so there was no evidence of his discovery.

When the slave ship arrived and requested Survey assistance, he was happy to help. They wanted to identify a member of the Guard located remote enough to be captured without witnesses. He had gleefully supplied Theron Stone's location. Unbeknownst to the odds makers, he had just eliminated a wild card. One more battle was all it would take. Now he just had to get ahold of more money. Knowing he had altered the odds gave him the confidence to gamble everything he could beg, borrow, or steal. His luck was definitely improving.

ABOUT THE AUTHOR

Tom Burrell resides with his wife in Northern California. When not writing, Tom is busy with their five children and five grandchildren. He has a degree in mechanical engineering from Cal Poly San Luis Obispo. Before becoming an author, Tom enjoyed a career in the electronic test and measurement industry.

Prior to becoming a responsible adult, Tom spent a decade of his youth wandering aimlessly, working a long list of jobs. These included lifeguard, swimming instructor, janitor, security guard, grill cook, painter, greenhouse worker, midnight shift convenience store clerk, residential liquor delivery driver, waiter, too many factory jobs to count, day laborer when immediate cash was required, and maker of handmade deer skin cowboy hats. These custom hats were sold by traveling around California to county fairs and other events where people tend to drink too much and make impulsive buying decisions.

If you enjoyed Pacifica, please consider giving a review. Feedback is a generous gift.

Books Two & Three of The Revelation Trilogy were released in the fall of 2024.

If you would like more information on T.E. Burrell and his books, please visit www.teburrellpubishing.com